Pra
Carlton

"Easily the craziest, weirdest, strangest, funniest, most obscene writer in America."
—*GOTHIC MAGAZINE*

"Carlton Mellick III has the craziest book titles... and the kinkiest fans!"
—CHRISTOPHER MOORE, author of *The Stupidest Angel*

"If you haven't read Mellick you're not nearly perverse enough for the twenty first century."
—JACK KETCHUM, author of *The Girl Next Door*

"Carlton Mellick III is one of bizarro fiction's most talented practitioners, a virtuoso of the surreal, science fictional tale."
—CORY DOCTOROW, author of *Little Brother*

"Bizarre, twisted, and emotionally raw—Carlton Mellick's fiction is the literary equivalent of putting your brain in a blender."
—BRIAN KEENE, author of *The Rising*

"Carlton Mellick III exemplifies the intelligence and wit that lurks between its lurid covers. In a genre where crude titles are an art in themselves, Mellick is a true artist."
—*THE GUARDIAN*

"Just as Pop had Andy Warhol and Dada Tristan Tzara, the bizarro movement has its very own P. T. Barnum-type practitioner. He's the mutton-chopped author of such books as *Electric Jesus Corpse* and *The Menstruating Mall*, the illustrator, editor, and instructor of all things bizarro, and his name is Carlton Mellick III."
—*DETAILS MAGAZINE*

"The most original novelist working today? The most outrageous? The most unpredictable? These aren't easy superlatives to make; however, Carlton Mellick may well be all of those things, behind a canon of books that all irreverently depart from the form and concepts of traditional novels, and adventure the reader into a howling, dark fantasyland of the most bizarre, over-the-top, and mind-warping inventiveness."
—EDWARD LEE, author of *Header*

"Discussing Bizarro literature without mentioning Mellick is like discussing weird-ass muttonchopped authors without mentioning Mellick."
—*CRACKED.COM*

"Carlton is an acquired taste, but he hooks you like a drug."
—HUNTER SHEA, author of *Forest of Shadows*

"Mellick's career is impressive because, despite the fact that he puts out a few books a year, he has managed to bring something new to the table every time… Every Mellick novel is packed with more wildly original concepts than you could find in the current top ten *New York Times* bestsellers put together."
—*VERBICIDE*

"Mellick's guerrilla incursions combine total geekboy fandom and love with genuine, unbridled outsider madness. As such, it borders on genius, in the way only true outsider art can."
—*FANGORIA*

Also by
Carlton Mellick III

Satan Burger
Electric Jesus Corpse (Fan Club Exclusive)
Sunset With a Beard (stories)
Razor Wire Pubic Hair
Teeth and Tongue Landscape
The Steel Breakfast Era
The Baby Jesus Butt Plug
Fishy-fleshed
The Menstruating Mall
Ocean of Lard (with Kevin L. Donihe)
Punk Land
Sex and Death in Television Town
Sea of the Patchwork Cats
The Haunted Vagina
Cancer-cute (Fan Club Exclusive)
War Slut
Sausagey Santa
Ugly Heaven
Adolf in Wonderland
Ultra Fuckers
Cybernetrix
The Egg Man
Apeshit
The Faggiest Vampire
The Cannibals of Candyland
Warrior Wolf Women of the Wasteland
The Kobold Wizard's Dildo of Enlightenment +2
Zombies and Shit
Crab Town
The Morbidly Obese Ninja
Barbarian Beast Bitches of the Badlands

FULL METAL OCTOPUS

CARLTON MELLICK III

ERASERHEAD PRESS
PORTLAND, OREGON

ERASERHEAD PRESS
205 NE BRYANT
PORTLAND, OR 97211

WWW.ERASERHEADPRESS.COM

ISBN: 978-1-62105-316-3

Copyright © 2021 by Carlton Mellick III

Cover art copyright © 2021 by Ed Mironiuk
www.edmironiuk.com

Printed in the USA.

AUTHOR'S NOTE

Hi. How's it going?

Is everything okay with you?

I hope everything is okay with you.

I guess everything is okay with me, too, but not really sure.

I'm writing you from the year 2020, in the middle of the Covid-19 pandemic. By the time you read this, it should all be over. Is it over? I hope it's over. Or maybe the virus has mutated into a new strain and created a twenty-seventh wave. Nah, I'm sure that didn't happen. I'm sure everything is fine. I am optimistic that by the time this book is released everything will be alright or at least be on the road to being almost alright.

It's been a long year. I mostly have just been staying home, reading books, playing video games, and trying not to gain too much weight with slight to moderate success. It's been okay. What I haven't been able to do much of is writing. It's difficult to write with even a small amount of stress, anxiety, or insecurity, so this has been a really problematic year for getting things done. Not only have I been anxious, but everyone I know has been completely batshit unstable and I'm very susceptible to the emotions of people around me. I have started about five different books that I gave up on after just a chapter or two, which is a failure that's only happened once before in my 15+ years as a professional writer. I hear that a lot of my author friends are also in the same boat. You'd think that having a year clear of social engagements would make it a whole lot easier to accomplish a lot of work, but nope. Didn't happen that way.

Anyway, I knew the easiest way to get into writing and actually finish what I started would be to write something fun and pulpy. Something like Armadillo Fists, Warrior Wolf Women of the Wasteland, or Clownfellas. What I really wanted to write was something like Clownfellas. If I owned the rights to the Clownfellas universe (I don't, long story) I would have written a sequel novella or two. Instead, I decided to write this book, which is similar to Clownfellas except that instead of being a mafia story set in a world where a race of clowns exist, it's a mafia story set in a world where different races of fairy creatures exist. Although it seems simple enough of a premise, I've never seen it done before and there are tons of directions I could take with this universe. There's a good chance that I'll want to explore this world again if people like it enough. Perhaps I could even do a six-part series like I did with Clownfellas. We'll have to see. If you like this book be sure to let me know what you think and I'll consider writing more *Full Metal* books in the future.

So here it is, my sixty-second book release. I hope it provides you with the much-needed escapism that it provided me.

—Carlton Mellick III, 12/17/2020 2:26am

CHAPTER
ONE

Eliot doesn't want anyone to know that he's a fairy. Not on the side of town he lives on. Just being a fairy makes him an easy target. Too many dangerous elements in his area that it's not very safe no matter what your race, but fairies are especially vulnerable. They're small in stature, no bigger than a twelve-year-old human girl when fully grown, even among the largest of them. And they are never very strong no matter how much they work out at the gym. Their bodies are incapable of packing on much muscle or fat. They have thin bird-like bones which break easily under even the lightest of pressure. They have soft, delicate flesh that bruises even from gently bumping into someone while passing them on the sidewalk after work.

At twenty-two years old, Eliot is barely five feet tall, and that's only while he wears his high-heeled combat boots and after he spikes up his naturally pink hair as high as it will go. He has seventeen tattoos and wears chains for belts, piercings on his lips and septum, and studded leather wristbands, all in order to come across as more manly and intimidating. But at best all he can hope to accomplish is to be mistaken for one of the local juvenile delinquents that most people in the neighborhood prefer to avoid. This is good enough for Eliot. If he can get people to ignore him, at least he will be safe.

He has a beautiful pair of emerald green butterfly wings with radiant pink and purple spots that he wishes he could exhibit in their full glory wherever he goes, but then he would just be asking for trouble. Even the police would blame Eliot if he was attacked around here. They would say that he should have known better, that of course he would attract the wrong kind of attention with his wings on display like that, wings as colorful and glittery and dazzling as his are. So wherever he goes, Eliot has to hide his wings under his thick black hoodie, tucking them into the back of his baggy cargo pants like their beauty is something to be ashamed of.

It's extremely uncomfortable for Eliot to go around with his wings squished and crumpled up like this, but he knows that it's much better than the alternative. As a fairy, Eliot is constantly harassed by everyone who crosses his path. The second they see his wings it's open season on him. Everyone wants a piece of fairy flesh. It doesn't matter what gender the person is. Both men and women are irresistibly drawn to Eliot regardless of sexual orientation. They follow him wherever he goes, through grocery store aisles, across parking lots, even into his apartment building, desperate to get his attention and ask for his phone number, hoping to get a shot at him, wishing more than anything for a chance to have a sexual encounter with someone of fairykind.

Because fairies are widely considered the prettiest of all the races, it makes perfect sense for people to be attracted to them and want to date them over anyone else in town. But the problem is that fairies have a reputation for being total sluts that are open to having sex with anyone, anywhere, anytime. All you have to do is ask them and they'll agree. But this is a complete myth perpetuated by stereotypes in film and television. The idea of the sexually promiscuous fairy has been around for ages and the vast majority of people believe it to be true without question. If you're a fairy and someone asks you for sex, they expect you to say yes. If you reject them, they'll get confused and upset. Sometimes they'll become angry or violent. It is a constant problem that forces most fairies to fear leaving their homes at night and hide their wings in public.

But sexual harassment isn't the biggest danger that fairies face when venturing into the streets. The sex slave trade has been booming in recent years and fairies are the prime targets. One wrong encounter and Eliot could find himself shipped off to some foreign country, forced to spend the rest of his life in sexual servitude. It is the thing that all of fairykind fears more than anything. It is why some fairies, such as Eliot, have been forced to take desperate measures in order to protect themselves from those who wish them harm.

The streets of the red-light district are lined with birdcages, black wrought iron enclosures that dangle from street posts and overhangs, swaying gently in the pungent breeze coming in from the highway. The fairy girls contained within come in all shapes and sizes and colors. There's a tall slender fairy with white moth-like wings and long platinum blonde braids, dangling her legs through the bars of her cage and humming like a bird that's trying to forget. A big-eyed fairy with blue wings and a matching blue pixie haircut rests her chin in her hands with a hauntingly fake smile spread permanently across her puppet-like face. The one with swooping pink hair and rainbow-colored wings whispers quietly to herself while curled in a fetal position, rubbing her thighs in an attempt to warm her bikini-clad body in the fifty-degree weather.

The cages are only just large enough to contain them, but far too small for them to move around much, too confining for them to stand up or lie down or sleep. Many of their wings have been sliced and frayed so that they can't fly away whenever their cages are opened. Those with wings left intact are adorned with fancy choke collars and leashes, perfect for a customer who prefers to lead a fairy like a child with a balloon all the way up to his hotel room bed.

The enslaved fairies sit up there, day in and day out, only freed from their cages to tend to their clients. They are like broken dolls. Pretty and delicate, but hollow within. Their spirits long left this world. Most of them are hooked on blue heroin, no longer caring about anything but losing themselves in that euphoric azure high. Others have long lost their minds and don't even realize where they are anymore.

As Eliot skateboards down the street, his pointed ears and insect-like antennae hidden beneath his hood, he makes eye contact with many of the fairies caged along the block. They can tell that he is one of them just by his smell and a specific twinkle in his eyes, but they don't speak a word of it. They don't want him to become a target of their captors and coerced into sharing their fate. But they also don't ask for his help. As someone who empathizes with them more than anyone in the city, Eliot would be the perfect person to help set them free. But they've long stopped caring about their own wellbeing. They wouldn't even know what to do with their lives even if they were to be set free.

Eliot doesn't like taking this route to the tattoo shop, but sometimes he feels like he has to in order to remember and appreciate the freedoms he still possesses. Even with his shitty rundown studio apartment, even with his dead-end jobs and abusive relationships, at least he is still free. At least he isn't in a cage and sold as a product in order to line the pockets of scumbags and criminals. At least his wings have not been clipped. At least he's still beautiful, even if his beauty is only allowed to shine when he's safe behind closed doors.

There are more than just fairies for sale in the red-light district. Prostitutes of all varieties can be found here. They line the streets, spread out a few women per block, smoking black weed cigarettes, waiting for their next customer. Elf girls staring everyone down with their deep silver eyes, silver hair combed to uniform perfection, glowing blue tattoos beneath their fishnet stockings. Harpy girls perched on balcony railings with their deep red feathers fluffed out, cooing and cawing, dropping white bird shit on those who ignore their solicitations. Bare-chested centaur women with saddles on their backs, clop-clopping back and forth on the sidewalk, charging fifty bucks for a lusty horseback ride.

Although prostitution isn't legal in this county, the cops don't do anything to stop it in this neighborhood. This is Sylph territory. The only police here are just as corrupt as the gangsters who run it. No one of fairykind would choose to venture into this part of the city if they had any good sense whatsoever, but Eliot just can't help himself. The tattoo shop that's located here is worth risking his life for. The area could be a war zone or on fire or the epicenter of a deadly plague and he'd still come.

Eliot is obsessed with getting tattooed. It is the one thing in his life that brings him real happiness. He works three jobs and saves up all of his money just to get more tattoos. He visits the tattoo shop at least once a week and during the days he's not getting tattooed he stares in the mirror, admiring the work on his body, fantasizing about what wonderful designs will adorn the empty sections of his skin.

But he doesn't want to be tattooed by just anyone. Oona is the only person he'll allow to put ink into his skin. She's a phenomenal artist, the best of anyone he's ever seen. She understands putting art on flesh in a way that goes beyond skill or talent. Her tattoos feel alive on your body, like they're injected with a part of her soul. But she doesn't have a whole lot of clients. Maybe because she's a woman in a male-dominated field or maybe because her shop is located in such a dangerous neighborhood. It also probably doesn't help that she's an octopus who insists on using ink produced from her own body whenever she works. Besides the deep racism felt towards those of merkind, the idea of having an octomaid's ink permanently embedded in your flesh is something that even the most enlightened of people find too disturbing a thing to go through with.

Eliot arrives at his destination and stomps his skateboard up in the air, catches it and tucks it under his arm. He's at the entrance of a notorious strip club called the Snake Pit known for its reptilian dancers and underworld clientele. Although most people avoid this place, it is actually the closest thing to a safe haven for Eliot in this whole neighborhood. It is a place where he can let his guard down and relax. The only place he's allowed to be himself.

One of the bouncers, an overly-muscled lizard-man, nods at Eliot and waves him through. Inside, crowds of crooked businessmen in crocodile suits chuckle amongst themselves in clouds of red smoke. Lamia dancers curl their snake bodies up stripper poles, flickering their long, forked tongues at the men lining the stage. A dragonian waitress blows fire to ignite a round of strong drinks before serving them to a table of rowdy ogres. Even this early in the evening, the place is bustling with activity.

Eliot takes off his hoodie and extends his wings. They billow out from his backless *Scum Punks* t-shirt and glitter in the neon lights. The instant he spreads them out, he feels everyone's eyes lock onto them, mesmerized by their majestic beauty. Ever since he was a kid, Eliot has had the most beautiful wings of any fairy he's ever known. His parents always thought that he should become a famous model with wings so pretty. Fairies, even more than elves, are always in demand in the fashion industry. Maybe he would have been really successful if he'd chosen that path in life.

Eliot stretches his wings. They are sore from being compressed inside his clothes all day and it feels good to free them and let them hang out. He flaps them a few times to straighten out the creases, bringing them back to their original shape. The strip club patrons behind him grow creepy smiles on their faces as they are fanned by his gorgeous wings. He can feel their eyes undressing him, wanting to reach out and grab his butterfly parts, caress them against their hairy, sweaty bodies. But he just ignores them and moves on.

Because his shirt is sleeveless, he's able to exhibit the tattoos down his arms. To Eliot, his tattoos are even more beautiful than his wings. They are black and gray fish designs, all Oona's original artwork. The second the customers see the illustrations, they keep their distance. Everyone who comes here on a regular basis knows Oona's work when they see it. They don't want to fuck with anyone that she's tattooed. It's like he's been branded as Oona's property and if they mess with him, they mess with her. And nobody wants to mess with Oona. She intimidates the hell out of people. An octomaid with six-inch talons and nine-foot tentacles born in the darkest depths of the ocean is not the kind of person you want on your bad side. Like most deep-sea merfolk, Oona is viewed as more of a demon than a civilized being. Savage and cold-blooded. She can make even the biggest and toughest of thugs feel small and helpless with a single look of her black menacing eyes.

But not everyone in the club is familiar with Oona's tattoos. Those who aren't regulars or who don't understand who's who in the world of skin art just see him as another tattooed stripper. With his big colorful wings and all that skin showing, they think he's fair game. These are the only people who give Eliot trouble in the Snake Pit. Luckily, the bouncers here protect him just as loyally as they would one of the dancers.

Eliot makes eye contact with someone across the room. A young elf in an expensive white suit with turquoise-colored hair styled in a stupid-looking swoop that is in fashion among elves these days. He winks and smiles at Eliot, flashing him a wad of cash. Eliot's never seen this guy here before. He is definitely a new customer and seems to be an especially obnoxious one at that. He sits at a table with a couple of his douchebag elf friends with equally stupid swoop hairstyles, only one has bronze-colored hair and the other's is silver. They drink pink cocktails and smoke red hot cigarettes, acting like they own the place. Lamia dancers in gold chainmail bikinis sit in their laps, their snake bodies wrapped around them, the looks in their eyes as if they wish they could be anywhere else but in their company. The rattlesnake girl with brown and gray-striped scales sitting in Silver Hair's lap rattles her tail frantically as if instinctually sensing danger, even though there's enough poison in her to kill him instantly if she decided to bite him in the neck.

Of all the races in the city, elves are the worst. Especially male elves. They're the most entitled, self-centered pricks Eliot's ever known. They think so highly of themselves, like they're the richest, smartest, and most attractive of all the species in the city. They think they own everything and everyone. Eliot can't stand them. They're even worse than humans. As a fairy, Eliot gets harassed by them more frequently than any of the other races combined.

Turquoise Hair tries to get Eliot's attention, waving him over. He pushes the coral snake girl out of his lap and makes room for Eliot, patting his thighs as if he wants the fairy to come sit. When Eliot breaks eye contact and turns away, the elf stands up and moves in closer.

Trying to avoid an unpleasant confrontation, Eliot flaps his wings and leaps into the air. He soars over the crowd of people, his wings drawing even more attention as he flutters like a butterfly through the colorful stage lights. Moving to the far side of the club, he lands on a barstool between two lamias, fanning them with puffs of air as he gets into his seat.

The two girls are excited when they see Eliot next to them. They are twin red racer snake girls that he sees frequently on his visits to Oona's tattoo shop. They smile so widely that they expose their long white fangs and flick their snake tongues at him.

"Oh, hi Eliot!" they cry out to him in unison.

Tiki and Taka are always really friendly to Eliot when he comes to the Snake Pit. They always make him feel happy and welcome. They treat him like their adorable little brother.

"How have you been, fairy friend?" Tiki says, squeezing his shoulder.

"Your wings are so pretty today!" Taka says, flickering her tongue at his glittery emerald wings.

"Thanks…" Eliot says, blushing a little.

Taka caresses his right wing, admiring its beauty, sending a shiver up his spine. Normally Eliot doesn't like it when people touch his wings, but the red racer twins are different. They are really nice and unthreatening, and he knows they're just being playful. Besides, he kind of likes the attention. Tiki and Taka are two of the cutest lamias in the club and are always full of enthusiasm and happy energy. Everyone just loves them. They are also two of the best dancers. They go on stage as a single act, entwining themselves together into a sexy knot that drives the customers wild.

"Let me buy you a drink," Taka says. "Flower nectar and vodka, right?"

"Sure…" Eliot says.

Everyone thinks fairies always drink flower nectar. It's one of the many stereotypes that film and television perpetuates, but Eliot doesn't hold it against Tiki and Taka. They are innocent when it comes to this kind of thing and don't really mean any harm. Personally, Eliot would have preferred a mint julep, but since the twins are paying, a flower nectar drink is fine. Who doesn't like flower nectar, anyway?

"Thanks, Taka," Eliot says.

When the drink comes, Eliot takes a sip and his antennae straighten on his forehead from the strength of the alcohol.

The Snake Pit always serves the strongest drinks in the neighborhood. With his body size, Eliot doesn't need too much to get drunk. So he sips slowly, just enough to get a good buzz and then pushes the drink aside for a while.

"It's so good to see you again!" Tiki says, even though they just saw him a few days ago. "We've missed you so much!"

"It's good to see you, too," Eliot says.

A smile widens on Eliot's face. It doesn't take much for the twins to cheer him up. He doesn't have too many people that are happy to see him these days, especially people who aren't trying to have sex with him.

"So are you getting tattooed again?" Taka asks. "What are you getting next?"

Eliot shrugs. "I don't know. I let Oona do whatever she wants. But she's going to be working on something new on my lower abdomen."

He lifts his shirt and shows the blank patch of skin below his belly button.

Tiki smiles and says, "That's going to be so hot." She rubs the skin he's showing with her scaly fingers, causing him to squeeze his thighs together in embarrassment. "I can't wait to see it when it's done."

Then she wraps her tail around Eliot's barstool, trying to pull him closer, flicking her tongue against his neck as she examines his tattoo work. Whenever they're working, Tiki and Taka are always in a flirtatious mood. Not just because he's a fairy and they are obviously attracted to him, but because it's expected of them in their line of work. It's almost like they are just practicing on Eliot for when a real customer comes to get their business.

"Taka got a tattoo the other day," Tiki says. "It's so amazing! You're going to love it!"

Eliot looks at Taka. She leans in close, her dark red hair and red makeup match the snake scales on her arms and lower snake body.

"Yeah, check it out!" Taka says. She uncoils her tail and places it on Eliot's lap. Then she points to a section of her red scales. "It's right here." But Eliot doesn't see any sign of a tattoo.

Taka laughs at Eliot's confusion.

"It's a secret tattoo," she says. Then she rubs her scales the wrong way, lifting them up, exposing an image of a pissed off lamia girl flipping the middle finger. "The artist tattooed the underside of my scales so you can only see it if you lift them up."

Eliot's eyes light up. It's an amazing tattoo. He never thought about getting tattooed in such a way. When he looks closer, he sees the words *fuck off!* printed beneath the image. He knows that lamias hate when men pet them the wrong way. They hate how it feels to have their scales lifted up in that direction. The tattoo was designed as revenge for any customer who mistakenly rubs her scales wrong. She can tell them to fuck off without getting in trouble from her boss.

"I love it," Eliot says. "It's so you."

Taka smooths her scales down, hiding the tattoo. "Thanks, fairy friend! I knew you'd like it."

"But it's not as good as your tattoos," Tiki says, stroking his tattooed arm. "Your tattoos are the best!"

Taka rubs her scaled tail. "I wish I had the money to get a tattoo from Oona. She charges so much. How do you afford it?"

Eliot shrugs. "I save up all the money I can, but I think it's worth it. Oona's the main reason why I get tattoos."

"Did she do all of your work?" Tiki asks.

Eliot nods. "Every single one. She's the person that got me into skin art in the first place. I couldn't imagine getting inked by anyone else."

"That's so cool!" Taka says. "I'm so jealous."

"Is it true that you're in love with Oona?" Tiki asks with a mischievous smile.

Eliot acts surprised. "What are you talking about? Who said that?" The twins laugh.

Tiki says, "There's a rumor that you're in love with Oona

and that's why you come to get tattooed by her so often. You've been coming here obsessively for months to get her tattoos. Some of the girls think it's because you like her."

Eliot can't stop blushing. It's true that he has a major crush on Oona. The first time he got a tattoo was because he saw her at a tattoo convention that his roommate dragged him to. He was so infatuated with her and her artwork that he had to get to know her better. The only reason he booked his first appointment with her was because he wanted to get closer to her. He wanted to find a way to get her phone number and ask her out. But he never had the courage to do it. He just got his tattoo and barely said a word to her. Then he set an appointment for a second tattoo. Then a third. Before he knew it, he was covered in her artwork.

"No, I don't like her like that," Eliot says, breaking eye contact to look down into his drink. "I just love her work…"

But the twins aren't buying it.

"It's true, isn't it?" Tiki says. "You're in love with Oona!"

Eliot holds up his hands. "I didn't say that…"

Taka wraps her arms around him and says, "Oh, you're so cute! You're like a lost puppy dog!"

Tiki hugs the other side of him. "Don't worry, your secret's safe with us!"

Then the girls giggle at each other over Eliot's shoulders. They pretend he's not there as Tiki says, "Wouldn't they make the cutest couple?"

"I know!" Taka says. "I've never seen a fairy with an octomaid before."

"Ooooh… It would be so adorable!"

"Imagine what their babies would look like?"

"Fairy wings with octopus tentacles! So cute!"

"It would be so great! This has to happen!"

"Eliot! You have to ask her out! Do it tonight!"

"Yeah, Eliot! You're perfect for each other!"

Eliot shakes his head. "I can't ask her out. She doesn't like me like that."

"Awwww!" the twins say in unison. Then they lay their heads on Eliot's shoulders.

"He's too shy!" Taka says.

"Oh Eliot, you're so sweet!" Tiki says, rubbing his thighs.

"Yeah, maybe you wouldn't work out as a couple."

"Yeah, Oona might be too big and scary for a sweet boy like you. She'd eat you alive."

The two snake girls give him a big hug and kisses on his cheek.

"It's okay, Eliot," Tiki says. "We still love you even if Oona doesn't."

"We'll give you a free lap dance later to make you feel better if you want." Then they giggle to each other and order another round of drinks for the three of them.

The twins always offer Eliot a free lap dance, but he's never taken them up on the offer. They don't seem to realize that it would be awkward for him to receive something like that from such close friends. He thinks it's nice of them to offer, but fairies get turned on too easily. If he became aroused enough to release his fairy pheromones it would surely turn into a sexual experience that would forever change their relationship. It's happened to Eliot too many times to count and the outcome has never been good. With his history of bad relationships, he knows that friendships are far more valuable than sexual experiences and he'd prefer to keep things the way they are.

Eliot changes the subject by thanking Taka for ordering him a second drink, even though he had no plans to finish the first.

Eliot feels a tap on his shoulder and turns around to see the turquoise-haired elf eying him with an intoxicated glare and a stupid smile on his face. Eliot groans at the sight of him.

"Hey fairy… You have super hot wings…" He nearly spills

his drink on Eliot as he leans closer.

"Yeah, I know," Eliot says, trying to dismiss him.

Guys like this usually get irritated when he agrees with their compliments rather than thanking them. It often leaves them feeling disarmed, not sure what to say next. They usually just say *well, you're not THAT hot* and then walk away. But this guy either didn't hear his comment or purposely ignored it.

He says, "Can I get a dance? I'd love to feel your wings flutter in my face." He rubs a finger down Eliot's bare back, between his wings.

Eliot pulls his wings away and gives him a look of disgust. "I don't work here."

"So what?" the elf says. "I've got money. I'll pay double. Triple."

The red racer twins see the look of distress on Eliot's face and try to bail him out. Taka leans toward the elf and wraps her scaled arm around his shoulder, flicking her tongue against his neck.

"I'll give you a dance, sexy," she says, a seductive look in her eyes.

But the elf just shoves her back and says, "Fuck no. I'm sick of you gross snake chicks. I want the fairy."

As the elf says this, Eliot feels his body changing. His penis sucks up into his body. His breasts grow, lifting his shirt up. His nipples expand, his hips widen, his facial features become more slender and feminine.

"God dammit!" Eliot screams, as he touches the swelling breasts on his chest. Then he shoves the elf and says, "Get the fuck away from me."

This is the worst part of being sexually harassed as a fairy. Whenever somebody approaches Eliot with a strong enough desire to have sex with him, his gender instinctually changes to suit the sexual orientation of the person who wants to mate with him. It's infuriating. Because Eliot identifies as male, he can't stand it when this happens. And the worst part is that the people hitting on him always see it as a sign that he's into them. Like he's personally responsible for altering himself to meet their needs. No matter what Eliot says, they always take it as a sign that he really does want to fuck them.

As Eliot changes, the elf gets turned on even more. He looks Eliot up and down, nods his head and licks his lips.

"Now we're talking," he says. "You're even hotter now. I definitely need to get to know you better."

As the guy starts grabbing at Eliot, Tiki waves over security. The largest reptilian bouncer doesn't waste a second. He comes in and gets between the elf and the fairy, pushing him back a few feet.

"Leave the fairy alone," the bouncer says. "Go back to your seat."

The elf gets annoyed. "Do you know who I am?" he yells at the bouncer. "You know what will happen if you fuck with me? Nobody tells me what to do."

The bouncer just keeps shoving him until he turns around and keeps walking.

"Yeah, yeah," the bouncer says. "Just cool down or I'll kick your ass out of here." They continue to argue with each other but are too far away for Eliot to hear.

As Eliot turns back to the bar, sulking at having his gender changed, Tiki and Taka rub his arms and try to calm him down.

"I'm sorry that happened to you, Eliot," Taka says, laying her head against his shoulder.

"That guy's been an asshole all night." Tiki wraps her tail around him and gives him a gentle squeeze. "Everyone's fed up with him."

It's not abnormal for Eliot to have his gender transformed like this. It happens at least once a week, especially in his apartment building or at one of his multiple day jobs where everyone knows he's of fairykind. But it's never happened at the Snake Pit before. It's beyond embarrassing to have his feminine side exposed to people who know him as male. A lot of people say they wish they had the ability to change genders, but it's not at all fun when you don't have control over the process. His gender is at the whim of other people's sexual desires. He doesn't like it one bit.

Although Eliot is embarrassed of his situation, trying to cover his breasts with his arms, closing his legs tightly, it seems that the red racer twins are kind of excited by his new look. Even though they try to comfort him, they can't help but be fascinated by his gender change.

"You look super cute as a girl, Eliot," Tiki says.

"You should be a girl more often," Taka says.

Eliot shakes his head. "I don't like it."

But the twins ignore him, admiring his new look. They pretend he isn't even there as they talk about him. Like he's their new doll or a cute little pet kitten.

"She's the prettiest fairy ever!" Tiki says.

"I know!" Taka cries. "Isn't she so adorable?"

Tiki says, "With those pink eyes and pink spiky hair, she's just the cutest! She just needs some makeup."

"Can we put makeup on you, Eliot?" Taka says, excitedly. "You'd be so cute with some green eye shadow to match your wings."

"I want to see him in a dress," Tiki says. "Can you try on one of our dresses? I have one backstage that might fit you."

Eliot shakes his head. "Come on, stop it. I'm not a girl. You're humiliating me."

"Ooohhh… she's even cuter when she's upset!" Taka says.

"I know! I just want to squeeze her all night!" Tiki says, tightening her tail around Eliot's waist.

Eliot lets out a sigh and shakes his head. Tiki and Taka always treat him this way, but it's even worse now that he's a girl. He finishes his drink and starts on the next one, even though he knows he can't drink too much. He's about to get tattooed soon and it's not good to do it with thinned blood. Oona might even turn him away if he shows up visibly intoxicated.

As Tiki squeezes him tighter, Eliot just says, "*He* not *she*." But otherwise lets them have their way with him.

Before Eliot finishes his second drink, Tiki and Taka are called to the stage and leave him behind. He's seen their act many times and loves watching them more than any of the other dancers, but he doesn't have time to sit around. He's got to get to his appointment with Oona. He hugs them goodbye and then heads to the women's bathroom. Although he identifies as a male, he knows he'll be safer there than in the men's room and he's used to switching bathrooms since his gender gets changed so frequently. It's easier for him to change back to male as long as he stays away from horny guys as much as he can.

The Snake Pit women's bathroom is also used as the changing room for the dancers. Several lamia girls are in here as Eliot enters, slithering around topless and snorting blue drugs. Their tails take up most of the floor, some of them more than twenty feet long, so Eliot has to step carefully, trying not to get tangled up as their snake halves coil around like they have minds of their own. The girls all go quiet and check out his wings as he approaches the mirror.

Unlike the elf, Eliot would welcome it if any of the snake girls hit on him right now. If one of them was interested in having sex with him then his gender might change back to male quicker. He doesn't want to face Oona as a girl. She probably wouldn't even recognize him. Besides, he's pretty sure she's not into girls and if she saw him as female she might think it was weird. He must turn back into a male as quickly as he can so that he doesn't keep her waiting.

But even though all the girls in the bathroom check him out and comment on how pretty his wings are, none of them are interested in having sex with him enough to get his gender to change back to normal. Either they prefer the sexual company of women or they are just not into having sex with anyone at the moment. Working as exotic dancers, they must be more used to turning people on than getting turned on themselves.

Eliot splashes cold water on his face, trying to calm down his hormones. He stands between two lamias who are applying green makeup to their faces in order to match their green scales. He doesn't recognize either of them. Even though the tips of their tails find their way to Eliot's ankle, coiling up his thigh to reach up to his wings, they don't say anything to him. They just chitchat with each other about some event they have to do on the other side of town later.

It takes several minutes, but eventually Eliot feels his breasts shrink and his penis grow back. He sighs in relief as his male features return to him. The girls in the room don't give him a second glance once they realize there's a man in the women's bathroom with them. Even as a male, fairies appear overly feminine and it's not uncommon for him to be treated as one of the girls despite what's between his legs. He's okay with it, though. He's back to his old self that's all that matters.

He exits the bathroom with caution, looking out for the turquoise-haired elf or any other guy who might harass him. He'll make it to his appointment as long as nobody hits on him again and turns him back into a girl. Once he's ready, he darts through the strip club, not stopping for a second. When someone gets in his way, he just jumps into the air and flies over them, but not so high that he attracts too much attention.

The back door of the club leads to a hallway with a few offices. One of them is Oona's tattoo shop. There's another entrance leading into the back alley that most of her customers use, but as a rule Eliot steers clear of back alleyways. He's had too many bad experiences to risk it. He just goes through the Snake Pit where the bouncers actually look out for him, unlike the cops would anywhere else in the neighborhood.

By the time Eliot reaches the door of the tattoo shop, he's

shaking. Being in Oona's presence always makes him nervous. But he's shaking more from anticipation than anxiety. He's been waiting all week for this moment. Any minute now and Eliot's going to be getting tattooed by the most beautiful woman he has ever seen.

CHAPTER TWO

The smell of Oona's tattoo shop fills Eliot's nostrils, overwhelming him with a pleasant combination of raw fish and tattoo soap. It puts a smile on his face every time he comes through the door. Eliot finds the smell of Oona's shop just as addicting as he does the act of getting tattooed. He sometimes arrives an hour early for an appointment just so he can bask in the lovely scent, breathing it in as one would a fresh cut rose. And after he goes home at night with a new tattoo on his arm, Eliot will often just inhale the smell for hours, remembering his time spent under Oona's needle, wishing the aroma would never disappear from his skin.

The front room is empty, which is just the way Eliot likes it. He prefers when it's just him and Oona. Not just because he gets awkward when creepy customers or other tattooists want to watch and drool over Eliot's inked skin, but because he likes the privacy. He likes having Oona all to himself.

"Is that you, Eliot?" Oona asks from the backroom. Her voice is as deep and serious as it usually is. She always speaks in a calm manner no matter the situation, very little emotion ever escapes her lips.

"Yeah," Eliot says.

He goes to the backroom to see Oona crawling out of the large aquarium that covers the back wall. She's topless and holding a live mackerel in her sharpened teeth. Eliot tries to avert his eyes as she climbs out of the fish tank, not realizing that he's caught her in such a compromising situation. But Oona doesn't seem to care. She casually puts her shirt back on and bites into the fish in her mouth. The mackerel flops around in her hand, still alive as she takes a few more bites, then she sets it down on a plate on the counter. The fish wiggles a few more times before it dies.

Oona uses the tank as a bed, a refrigerator, and a feeding trough. She needs to soak the octopus half of her body for at least ten minutes every hour, preferably with salt water. Eliot knows that she spends much of her free time soaking in the cold murky water of her aquarium, just lying in there and letting her mind go blank, remembering what life was like as a child in the ocean, swimming and eating and living like a creature from the depths. Oona also uses the fish tank to store her meals while working at the shop. Because she prefers the taste of live sea creatures, it's a perfect place to keep a few lunches alive and squirming for when she's ready to eat.

Eliot's so excited to see Oona, so excited to get tattooed, that his wings can't stop fluttering. They flap back and forth like he's getting ready to take off, blowing the punk band fliers on the wall behind him with such force that they almost rip off the thumbtacks holding them up.

Oona rubs down her wet blue mohawk, squeezing out the salt water. She's had a mohawk ever since Eliot's known her but he's never seen it standing up as it's supposed to. Because she soaks in her tank so often it's always wet and saggy, a curly mess on the top of her head.

"Take off your clothes," Oona tells him.

She always has Eliot strip down to his boxer briefs when tattooing him, even if she's just tattooing his arm or leg. She sees the art on his body as one complete piece and you don't paint a picture only looking at one section of the canvas at a time. She wants to see all of him, all her previous work and all the work she might do in the future. Although Eliot's shy and doesn't like to take off his clothes for anyone, he understands her process and doesn't want to ruin it. Besides, he's comfortable around Oona. He feels safe in her company. If any other tattooist asked him to take off his clothes, he would think they were being creepy assholes who just wanted to see him half-naked. But Oona isn't like that. She doesn't see Eliot as a sex object as most people do. She sees him as a canvas that she wants to fill. And Eliot loves the idea of being her canvas.

Eliot takes off his clothes as Oona finishes her lunch, head and all, leaving only a pile of bones on the plate. He watches her tentacles slithering across the linoleum floor, leaving a trail of fishy slime. He loves the way her tentacles look when they move, curling and twisting. He finds them erotic and beautiful. Most guys don't like octopus girls because they see the tentacles as phallic, like they've got a bunch of giant dicks attached to their body, but Eliot thinks that's ridiculous. He sees octomaid tentacles as feminine and pretty. He would date an octomaid in a second and never once think of her tentacles in a phallic way.

He wonders if octomaids feel the same way as he does. As a fairy, people always see his wings as cute and girly even though he sees them as masculine and powerful. He's very manly for a fairy. But compared to other races, he's effeminate. He wonders if Oona is sick of her tentacles being seen as overly masculine. He wonders if she wants someone to appreciate her as a beautiful woman. Although the thought of this makes Eliot happy, like maybe he can date an octomaid as perfect as Oona just by how he views her femininity, deep down he knows she wouldn't care. She couldn't give a shit one way or another how anyone felt about her. She's above all of that.

"Get on the chair," Oona says as she prepares the ink and needle.

Although Oona usually has ink ready to go, she must have run out earlier because she has to produce more ink from her body. She puts a vial under her tentacle and squirts it out like milk from an udder. It's fascinating for Eliot to witness. He's never seen it happen before. He's always loved the idea that she

33

tattoos him with ink from her own body, but he didn't realize the process was so intimate, maybe even sexual. Oona even moans as she squeezes, like she's masturbating right there in front of him. Eliot diverts his eyes, concerned that he might be witnessing something that he shouldn't be witnessing.

Eliot crawls up into the hydraulic chair, gently bending his wings back in such a way so that they will be comfortable behind him as he reclines. As he lies there in the cold vinyl chair, he quivers with anticipation. He can't wait to feel new ink going into his skin.

When Oona's ready, Eliot braces himself. She doesn't have to say anything before starting. She knows exactly what she's going to do. She rubs alcohol on the sensitive section of Eliot's skin beneath his belly button, pushing his pink boxer briefs down a few inches to have a larger surface area. The second she touches this part of his skin, Eliot immediately becomes erect, his penis lifting the crotch of his underwear up high enough that it's impossible to hide. This happens almost every time Eliot gets tattooed. Because he's a fairy, Eliot becomes aroused even by the gentlest touch. It's been a problem he's had to deal with ever since childhood. This is one reason why fairies are stereotyped for loving to have sex. It's not that they are down for having sex with anyone anytime, it's that they have extra sensitive nerve endings and are turned on easily. But just because they get aroused by the smallest touch, doesn't mean they want to have sex. It's a bodily function that Eliot has no control over. Even a pet cat rubbing against his leg can cause it. Even a cold breeze blowing through his wings. Even a tap on the shoulder by an old man trying to get by him on the subway. It's a part of fairy life that's more of a curse than anything. He's had to learn to live with random erections since he was young.

Oona surely has noticed that Eliot gets aroused by her touch, but she's never seemed to point it out or care very much. She's never reacted with disgust nor excitement. It's like she understands that it's just a natural bodily function and tolerates it in the same way she might a cough or a blink.

Despite how Oona's done well to ignore Eliot's erections in the past, she's never worked so close to his penis before now. It's definitely awkward for Eliot, but it doesn't seem to have any effect on Oona. She only cares about the art she's about to put on his body.

As she lifts the needle and examines her canvas, she sighs and shakes her head. She grabs Eliot's underwear by the waistband and shakes it.

She says, "I'm sorry, but these have to go."

Eliot panics a little. "Wait... what? My underwear?"

She responds with a cold calm voice. "Yeah, the design I have in mind needs to stretch down farther."

Eliot becomes flustered. "But then I'll be naked..."

He looks into her deep black eyes but she doesn't seem to care about his concern. She just sighs and says, "I'll also have to shave you."

Although Eliot didn't think he was going to have any of his private areas tattooed today, he guesses Oona has other plans. Ever since their first tattoo session, Eliot agreed to let her tattoo him in any way she sees fit. She gives him a discount to be able to tattoo him however she wants. He's a pet project for her, different than the strippers and gangsters she usually tattoos. She's allowed to be creative, do whatever she wants to any part of his body if it meets her artistic desire, so if she wants to tattoo in his pubic region he's going to let her do it.

Eliot reluctantly takes his underwear off. Embarrassed of his erect penis being on display, he tries bunching his underwear up and placing it on top of his crotch to cover it up. But the underwear almost instantly rolls off his thigh onto the floor. Completely exposed to the woman he has a crush on, Eliot just takes a deep breath and lets it happen. It's a good thing he had those drinks before getting tattooed or else he would have had a complete panic attack. But even with the alcohol, Eliot still feels incredibly vulnerable and uncomfortable. Luckily Oona notices his discomfort.

"Here," she says, pulling out a washcloth-sized towel and laying it over his penis. "Better?"

Eliot nods. "Thanks."

But he's not sure what's more embarrassing for him, to get covered up or to be left naked. He'd rather be known as the kind of person who's confident in his nudity than ashamed of it. Either way, he's able to relax a little better with the towel, even as small as it is.

She shaves off his pink pubic hair with a blue disposable razor. She does it so quickly that Eliot doesn't even realize it's happening until she's already halfway finished. Fairies don't grow much body hair compared to most of the other races, so she's able to get it all off with five quick strokes of the razor. Once there's just a dusting of stray pink hairs, Oona wipes the area clean, leaving Eliot as bald as a prepubescent boy.

When the needle starts buzzing, all of Eliot's nerves tense up at the same time. Even though fairies have a stronger sense of touch and feel pain more acutely than other races, Eliot rather likes the sensation of being tattooed. Maybe because Oona is the one doing it, maybe because he has a bit of a masochistic side, but the pain is not nearly as bad as he thought it would be before he got his first tattoo.

Oona's tentacles wrap around Eliot's body as she begins. The appendages curl up his chest and around his stomach, holding him in place so that she can do her work without his movements getting in her way. The cold slime coats his chest as the tentacles tighten around him. He feels fastened to the chair, like wearing a seatbelt, the suction cups adhering to his body so tightly that his skin turns white around them. Like every time he gets tattooed, Eliot will go home covered in red circles from where her suction cups had secured him. But he kind of likes the look of them, like they are love bites she left on his body to keep other women away from him.

Eliot loves the look in her eyes when she works on him. She

narrows her vision, intently focusing on his skin, as she buries her ink into his body. She doesn't sketch out her art before getting started as she would with any other customer. She tattoos freeform with Eliot, carving out an image straight from her imagination. Most people wouldn't allow a tattooist to do such a thing, but Eliot trusts her. Every tattoo on Eliot's body has been perfect. She's never messed up and needed to tattoo over anything. Her freeform art never ceases to be amazing. In fact, Eliot thinks his skin art is her best work. Something about letting her do anything she wants without his approval brings out another side of her. She's able to let her creativity flow right from her mind into Eliot's flesh.

Eliot's biggest dream is to become Oona's masterpiece. Once his flesh is completely filled with her art, he hopes she views him as the greatest work of her career. He hopes she takes him to tattoo conventions to exhibit him to all the greats in the tattoo world, showing him off as the peak of her ability. Maybe then she'll fall in love with him. Even if it's just for the designs on his skin, Eliot would love for her to see him as more than just a client. He knows it's just a dream but it is the one thing that gets him through his day to day life. The thing that gives him hope.

The pain of the needles cutting into his skin causes Eliot to tense up. Her tentacles grip him tighter as he shakes, holding him in place as he clenches the arms of the chair.

"Doing okay?" she asks him.

He nods but doesn't say anything. She asks the question multiple times while he's being tattooed as standard procedure, but doesn't seem to care what his response is. She just wants to keep designing. She doesn't want to stop until the piece is finished. Eliot could be whimpering in pain and begging her to stop and she wouldn't even notice.

Once she gets in the zone, Oona forgets where she is. She loses herself in her art and her surroundings go blank. She doesn't even see Eliot as a living being anymore. It's just her ink and her canvas and that's all she can think about. Eliot can tell she's in the zone whenever her tentacles start moving on their own. They start writhing against Eliot's bare skin or curling around the chair or swaying in the air. It's like a musician instinctually tapping her foot or bobbing her head when playing a good rhythm.

Eliot wonders if she's this way with all of her clients or if it's just him. Nobody gives her permission to let loose on their bodies like he does. Despite her lack of emotion, she seems to love tattooing him. It's like it's the only time she's at peace in the world. Eliot tries to get a look at the work she's doing, but she covers it up with her free arm, blocking his view. She's like a child in art class who doesn't want anyone to see her drawing until it's completely finished.

Endorphins are flooding Eliot's system, both from the pain of the needle and the sensitivity of Oona's touch. Oona's never tattooed him in such a vulnerable part of his body before. The side of her hand is resting on his bald pubic area, just above his penis. She probably doesn't realize that she keeps inching closer and closer to it, probably forgot he even is a person with a penis. But the sensation is making Eliot squirm in his seat.

Eliot can't help but see this as a sexual experience. He actually prefers this over any time he's ever had sex in the past. He's been in relationships with many people of many different races but has never really enjoyed having sex with them. He usually was only in those relationships to fight off the loneliness. A few human girls when he was younger, an elf woman twice his age, a water nymph who always talked about herself and only wanted Eliot as a pretty accessory to impress her shallow friends. He even once dated a male dryad for a few weeks, just to try something new, spending most of his time as a woman for his partner's sake, but really didn't enjoy even a minute of it. Sex always felt cheap and empty, always about getting the other person off just to keep them happy and interested. But when he's being tattooed by Oona, it feels far more intimate and beautiful. He loves the feeling of her wrapped around him, inserting her ink into his body, transforming his flesh into a magnificent work of art. He'd rather experience this than any sex he's ever had in his life.

Eliot leans back, enjoying the sensation of her needle cutting into his skin. His senses are so heightened that he feels like he's about to have an orgasm at any second. His wings flutter behind his back and Oona's grip tightens against his body. He closes his eyes, stretching out his muscles, as Oona tattoos him at a furious pace. She's so absorbed in her work that she has no idea what she's doing to him. His fingers curl into tight little fists. His thighs squeeze together. He knows it would be beyond embarrassing if he actually had an orgasm right there on the spot, but he's not sure he's able to control himself this time. One of her tentacles is practically rubbing against his penis, nearly pulling the small towel away and grabbing hold of him. He doesn't want it to happen but he can't help but be overwhelmed by it all.

The tattoo shop door slams open and drunken laughter fills the front room. Oona breaks her concentration and pulls back from her work. Her needle stops its buzzing. Eliot's never seen emotion on her face before, but she is clearly annoyed by the interruption. It's just a slight curl on the side of her mouth, a narrowing of her eyes, but she's definitely not happy. Nobody would dare interrupt her during a session if they value their lives.

"We're not open," Oona yells.

They're in the next room, so Eliot can't tell who they are. They sound like a group of rowdy drunks from the strip club. They hoot and holler, ignoring Oona's comment. One of them knocks over what sounds like the bookstand full of tattoo portfolios. The others laugh and kick the binders across the linoleum floor.

"Oh, fuck no..." Oona says, uncurling her tentacles from Eliot's body and standing up.

When Eliot hears the elf's voice, he knows exactly who it is and why they're here.

"Where you at, fairy bitch?" the elf yells. "I wasn't done with you."

Eliot's breath freezes in his lungs and his heart pounds in his chest. His mind is still so clouded with endorphins that he isn't sure if this is really happening or not. He's in such a vulnerable position with his clothes on the other side of the room, only a washcloth covering his privates. He can't handle the thought of facing the creepy elf like this. He wants to run for his clothes, but the second he sits up Oona pushes him back down into place with just two fingers and a thumb.

The elves appear in the entryway of the room and Eliot goes into panic mode, trying to cover his body with his hands.

"There you are, Sexy," Turquoise Elf says, winking at Eliot. "I've been looking everywhere for you."

Before they can come all the way in, Oona spreads out her tentacles in an intimidating posture. They stretch out across the room and crawl up the walls, filling the area so that the elves don't have any space to get any closer, telling them to stay the fuck back without saying a word.

They don't take another step.

"Get out," she tells them. "I'm busy."

But the elves don't go. They only laugh when they see her, either too drunk or too stupid to be afraid. It takes a special kind of asshole to stand up to someone twice your size and snicker in their face. It's like they see themselves as the biggest badasses in town despite their lack of musculature. Males of elfkind have rather slender physiques, only appearing strong to the few races who are even more petite in stature, such as pixies and fairies.

"Holy shit..." Turquoise Hair says when he gets a good look at Oona, looking her body up and down. "So you're the octopus lady they kept talking about inside." He cracks a grin. "They were right. You *are* one scary bitch."

She raises her body up, standing a good foot and half over the trio of skinny elf pricks. They don't look her directly in the eyes, trying not to let her intimidate them. They just laugh off their fear and hold in place.

"You must be Niko, the Kaji brat," Oona says to Turquoise Hair. "What the hell do you want?"

Niko holds up his hands like he's an innocent passerby. "I'm just interested in getting a tattoo. They say you're pretty good."

Oona shakes her head. "I don't take walk-ins. Come back tomorrow and maybe we can schedule something."

Niko laughs in her face. "If you know who I am you know I don't wait for anything. If I want a tattoo I get a tattoo."

"I'm busy," Oona says.

Niko smiles and looks back at his two friends. "Of course. You can finish tattooing the fairy if you want. I'll stay and watch. I'd like to see you in action."

"I don't work that way."

The elf lifts his shirt and shows off the gun in his waist band. "I think you do now."

Oona glares at him. She doesn't acknowledge his gun. She just stares at him like she's about to strangle him to death. But when Eliot sees the weapon, he freaks out. He lifts himself up in the seat, gripping the armrests so tight that his glittery long fingernails dig holes into the vinyl. He's sure Oona will save him, though. She's the toughest person he knows. Even if they're armed, the elves stand no chance against her. She can wrap them up in her tentacles and break their necks faster than they can reach for their guns.

But she doesn't attack them. Oona just pulls her tentacles back and lets them enter the room.

"Fine…" she says, lowering her eyes. "You can watch. But if you get in my way I'll kick your ass out."

The elves giggle at her threat but don't say anything about it. Niko lowers his shirt and comes closer to Eliot.

"This is going to be fun," the elf says to him, placing his arm on the armrest next to his hand. "Your tattoos are hot."

Eliot pulls his arm away. He can't believe Oona's letting the elf get away with this. She's supposed to be the Demon of Grub Town. Nobody tells her what to do. He knows this has to be some kind of a trick.

But Oona doesn't seem concerned in the slightest. She goes back to the other side of the tattoo chair, picks up her needle and gets back to work. She turns the needle on and continues where she left off.

Eliot is not comfortable with this. He thought he had Oona's protection. It's why nobody ever messed with him in the Snake Pit. But he has no idea why she isn't standing up to these punks. Even the bouncers would have kicked them out of here by now. It seems all Oona really cares about is her art and this was the easiest way she could get back to her tattooing with the least amount of resistance. All she wants is to finish her piece, even if it's at the expense of Eliot's comfort and safety.

While Oona gets back into the zone, shading the piece on Eliot's lower abdomen, the three elves step in closer to leer at his naked body. Eliot's muscles tense up, feeling awkward being gawked at by the creepy men. He can feel their eyes scanning every inch of his body, enjoying the sight of him squirming under the needle. Maybe it's because they're watching him, maybe it's because Oona's taking out her anger at the elf on Eliot's body, but the pain is much worse than it usually is. It's even more painful than when she tattooed his spine between his delicate wings.

Niko licks his lips while Eliot is being tattooed. "I want to see your wings," he says. "Stop hiding them behind your back."

When Niko pinches an inch of his wing and tugs on it,

Eliot cries out. To make him stop he sits up and spreads out his wings, letting them fall down the sides of the chair so the elves can see them. This is enough for the elf to let go and Eliot is able to relax. He lets his wings sway a bit, giving them some air to breathe. Despite doing it on request, it feels better to let them go. He didn't realize they had been so cramped in their position until now.

"Oh yeah, there they are…" Niko says. "Those are the hottest fairy wings I've ever seen."

The other elves agree and come in to get a better look, basking in their glory.

This experience is not at all pleasurable for Eliot. He's long since lost his erection and no longer feels the sexual energy that overwhelmed him before the elves interrupted the session. Getting tattooed is such a beautiful sexual experience normally, but now it feels more like he's being molested than making love. The presence of the elves have ruined everything.

But at least Eliot is able to see the tattoo Oona is creating. She isn't covering it as she normally does, tattooing as if it's an exhibition, showing her work off to the onlookers as she immerses herself in her art. She wipes away Eliot's silver fairy blood after every line she cuts. He's bleeding a lot more than he usually does, maybe because he had too much alcohol or maybe because his nervousness is causing his heart to pump his blood too rapidly through his body. Either way, the paper towels coated in his shiny silver blood are beginning to stack up.

Niko hovers over Eliot, swaying back and forth from having too much to drink. But no matter how dizzy he gets, he won't take his eyes off of the fairy. He examines every inch of him, holding out his hand as if he's about to touch him.

"Man, your tattoos are sexy as hell," Niko says. "What I wouldn't do to have them pressed up against my body…"

Eliot cringes and inches away from him in the chair.

Before Niko can touch him, Oona puts a tentacle in his

face and says, "Keep your distance. I'm working here."

Niko pulls back his hand. "I'm not touching anyone."

Oona keeps going. She's so close to finishing that she doesn't want to spend a second more dealing with the elven creeps. When Eliot gets a good look at the tattoo, he realizes it's one of the best pieces she's done on him. It's the image of a coiled eel that connects to the tattoo on his stomach above his belly button. The eel design fills his lower abdomen and ends in his pubic region near his penis. The head of the eel extends toward the base of his shaft, as though Oona plans to tattoo his penis into a small fish that the eel is about to swallow as its prey. The concept is kind of embarrassing to Eliot, but he can already imagine it will make an interesting work of art. It's just not the kind of thing Eliot expected Oona would create. She's usually much more subtle than that. Perhaps he just has to wait for her to finish the whole piece before he jumps to conclusions. The final product has always been far more amazing than he can ever imagine.

But despite how much he wants to see the finished version of Oona's tattoo, he can't help but hope that she never stops. He wants the elves to get bored and leave on their own, so he and Oona can get back to where they were before the creeps showed up. But no matter how long it takes, the elves won't leave. Eliot is paranoid about what will happen when Oona's done. Will they let him leave in peace? Or will they not give up until Eliot does whatever they say until they're satisfied? If Oona won't stop them, then Eliot has to get back to the Snake Pit as soon as possible so that the bouncers will protect him. And if that doesn't work, what then? Will they try to capture him and take him home against his will? Are they after him so that they can sell him into slavery? He won't let that happen. He'd rather die than be forced into that lifestyle. Trapped in a birdcage to decorate some scummy rich man's living room, a pretty little sex toy without any rights or privileges, it would be the worst thing that could ever happen to him. If Oona won't protect him, he'll have to do whatever it takes to protect himself.

Niko won't stop leering at Eliot, pressing his thigh against the fairy's right wing, trying to make eye contact no matter how much the fairy ignores him. Although the elf was mostly focused on watching Oona tattooing Eliot's pubic region, getting turned on by how the fairy squirmed at the pain, he's now lost interest in the tattoo work and just wants to eyeball the rest of the fairy's pretty little body. Although Eliot's not a Snake Pit stripper, the elves gawk at him as though he's the headlining entertainment of their evening. They can't get enough of him. It's like they've never been in the presence of a fairy before.

As the elf gets more turned on by Eliot's naked appearance, Eliot starts to feel his body changing again. His breasts swell out and his penis is sucked into his body, lowering the wash cloth covering his pubic region. This has never happened while Eliot's been tattooed before, so it throws Oona off her game. She pulls the needle back as his figure transforms in front of her. The area below his belly button stretches and expands, making space for a womb beneath his flesh. It changes the shape of her tattoo work, ruining the perfect design she was working on.

The elves freak out at the sight of Eliot's naked breasts expanding on his body, getting them even more turned on by the sight of him. As Eliot's body changes, his nudity becomes so uncomfortable that he whimpers out loud, even his whimpers take on a more feminine tone. He covers his breasts with his arms, trying not to let anyone see the tears forming in his eyes. He's absolutely humiliated by being transformed without clothes on, his nudity on full display for everyone to see. He hates the idea of the creepy elves seeing him in this state, but it's even worse having Oona see him in his feminine from. He never wanted her to see him as a woman. Because he has such a crush on her and wishes she would someday see him as a potential boyfriend, he's ashamed to expose this side of himself to her.

Oona glares at Eliot as if he's to blame for this. "What the hell's going on? Why are you a woman now?"

Eliot is confused that she has to ask. Everyone knows fairies switch genders against their will. She has to know why this is happening.

Her eyes turn to Niko. "Are you responsible for this?"

He laughs. "Sorry, I can't control how I feel. She's hot as fuck."

"You're going to have to leave, then. I can't work like this."

The elves boo her and urge her to continue.

"Keep going," says Silver Hair.

"This is just starting to get good," says Bronze Hair.

Niko just shakes his head and rests his hand on the gun in his pants. "We're not going anywhere."

Oona gives him a look like she's about to kill him. "Well, I need him to be a guy or I can't tattoo him properly. Either calm your hormones or get out."

Niko smiles. "Why don't you just leave the room for a few minutes and let her give me a blowjob? That will calm me down. I'm sure she'll transform back after that."

The room goes silent for a moment. Eliot looks around, wondering if he should make a run for the exit.

"Yeah, she should give us *all* blowjobs," says Silver Hair, then receives a high-five from the elf with bronze-colored hair.

Oona doesn't break eye contact with them. For a second, Eliot thinks she's going to take Niko up on the offer. Since she seems to care more about her art than she cares about Eliot's wellbeing, it would make sense for her to see this as a good compromise. But she doesn't agree to the proposal.

"No, get out," she tells him.

Niko just smirks at her. He looks back at his friends and then pulls out his gun and points it in Oona's face.

"No," he says. "*You* get out."

46

Oona narrows her eyes at him.

"It's my birthday today," Niko says. "Why are you trying to ruin my birthday? All I want for my birthday is a blowjob from a pretty little fairy girl. Is that too much to ask?"

Oona's tentacles unravel from the tattoo chair and spread out across the floor. She doesn't say anything. She doesn't even look at the weapon in the elf's hand, still looking him in the eyes.

Niko's voice changes to a more serious tone. "Today my father promoted me. I'm finally considered a man in his eyes. He's never been more proud." His voice is a little shaky, as though he's about to cry. He wipes his eye with his free hand just before a tear begins to form. "This is supposed to be the best day of my life, the moment I've been waiting for since I was a kid. Why do you have to make it so complicated?"

The elf pauses for a moment. His lips are trembling.

"Look, I'm not an asshole," he says. "I have money." He pulls out a large wad of bills and drops it onto Eliot's stomach. "That's three thousand dollars. She can have it all. It'll be the most expensive blowjob I've ever paid for. You can take a cut if you want. I know you're a big deal around here. I don't want to cause your boss any trouble. All you have to do is give me this. All I want is for my night to end with my dick between this fairy's lips and I'll leave you both alone."

Oona curls her mouth downward a little and takes a breath.

She points down at Eliot. "It's his call."

When her eyes meet his, Eliot is still in a state of panic. He opens his mouth but can't get any words out.

"I won't judge you if you decide to take the money," she tells him.

But Eliot has no intention of doing it for any price. The emotional scar alone isn't worth it, and Eliot knows the elf will want even more than a blowjob for that kind of money. He's sure, if the elf gets his way, it will end with Eliot in a birdcage.

Oona looks down at Eliot and says, "So do you want to or not?"

Eliot can't answer. He can only look her in the eyes, tears rolling down his cheeks. He shakes his head once, so rapidly that the elves won't notice, begging her to help him using only his eyes.

She understands immediately and nods her head. Then she looks back at Niko and tells him, "He's not interested."

Niko erupts with frustration. "Are you fucking kidding me? I'm willing to put down that kind of money and you spit in my face for it?"

Oona slaps the wad of cash off Eliot's belly and it scatters on the slime-caked linoleum.

"Fuck it," Niko says. "I don't care what the fairy wants. How much is it going to take *you* to back off? I can double that amount, triple it, if you walk away. Give us your shop for an hour and we'll be all good."

Oona doesn't give in and stares him down.

"I know you like money," the elf says. "You wouldn't charge such crazy prices for your tattoos if you didn't."

"I charge that much to scare people away, not because I want the money," she says. "I only tattoo serious clients."

Niko screams out in frustration. "Are you fucking serious? Do you really want to go to war over this? Because that's what's going to happen. Do you really think your boss would agree with your decision? You think she'd be happy with you protecting this piece of ass?"

"Get out," Oona says. "This is your final warning."

Niko can't help but laugh. "Are you fucking kidding me?"

"Now."

"Are you willing to die over this, you crazy bitch?"

"If you're going to shoot just do it already."

Niko rolls his eyes. "Fine. If that's how you want to do this, I don't have any choice but to—"

Before he can finish, a tentacle whips through the air so fast that Niko doesn't even see it coming. It coils around his gun hand and twists it back, then he gets slapped across the face with another tentacle. The weapon falls to the floor.

"What the fuck!" Niko screams, coiling backward with his hand covering his eye. He's so drunk that he can't even tell exactly what she did to him. All he knows is that his eye is bleeding from the slap. He touches his face and looks down at the silver blood. "You fucking bitch…"

The other two elves reach for their guns, but Oona pulls their legs out from under them. Bronze Hair's skull hits the linoleum so hard a cracking noise echoes in the room. Silver Hair catches himself, but another tentacle wraps around his waist and throws him against the wall, knocking the wind out of him.

Eliot jumps out of the chair and into the air, his wings fluttering to keep him afloat. But with such a low ceiling he's not able to get very high. The small towel falls to the floor, leaving him even more nude than before. He covers both his crotch and his breasts with his hands as he hovers, not sure what else to do but to try to hide the exposed parts of his body from the creepy elves.

"You're so dead!" Niko screams at the octomaid.

Before he can recover his weapon, Oona wraps a tentacle around Niko's neck and lifts him into the air. She stares him in the eyes as she chokes the life out of him. He struggles. His legs kick. His fingers grip her tentacle.

He chokes out the words, "Kill this… ugly freak…"

But Niko doesn't die fast enough. While she is preoccupied with him, Silver Hair collects himself and puts a gun to the back of her head. She pauses the second she feels it against the bald part of her scalp, but she doesn't let Niko go.

"Pulling the trigger won't save him," Oona says. "You won't be able to get him out of my death grip."

"Just put him down," says Silver Hair, trying to catch his

breath. "He's the son of Shino Kaji. You don't want to do this." His voice is shaky, as though he's more afraid of what will happen to him if anything happens to his boss's son.

As he says this, the bronze-haired elf gets to his feet, blood dripping from his scalp. He steps back, out of the reach of Oona's tentacles, and points his gun at her. There's nothing she can do to stop him.

Niko's face turns blue. He's losing the strength to even kick his legs as the octomaid lifts him even higher off the ground, moving him away from the hydraulic chair so that he can't use it to prop himself up.

"If he dies you die," says Silver Hair. "Let him go."

Oona shrugs. "Dying doesn't mean much to me at my age. I'm an octomaid. We rarely live past thirty and I'm already twenty-seven. I'm already nearing the end of my lifespan. Get out and maybe I'll let him go."

The elves don't leave, nor do they shoot, so Oona doesn't let go of her grip on Niko's neck. As Eliot flutters in the air, backing himself into the corner of the room, he can't tell if Oona is bluffing or telling the truth. He always thought of her as a survivor. Deep sea merfolk are always more instinctual than emotional and nothing is stronger than the instinct for survival. He's sure she has no intention of dying here.

As Oona is distracted by the guns pointed at her, the turquoise-haired elf pulls a switch blade from his pocket and stabs into her tentacle. He cuts halfway through it before she lets him go and pulls her appendage back. Purple blood splashes across the tattoo chair, but she doesn't cry out. Niko falls to his knees and coughs, gasping for air, pointing his knife upward to keep her back.

"Grab her…" Niko commands his friends.

Silver Hair puts his arm around Oona's neck, pressing his gun tight to her temple. Her tentacles coil up his legs, around his waist, but he doesn't let go. Bronze Hair rushes her and kicks her in the stomach. The second his foot makes contact, she pukes up her fish dinner onto his pant leg. Octomaids don't have bones so their flesh is soft and spongy. Even their human halves are made of cartilage instead of bone. Just one kick in a vulnerable area and her tentacles go limp. She slides down until her crotch splats on the floor.

While Oona struggles with the two elf thugs, Eliot tries to escape. He doesn't know what else to do. If he flees maybe they will follow him and leave Oona alone. He'd rather they do whatever they want to him than see them hurt her anymore.

As Eliot goes for the door, Niko lunges at him and grabs his leg, clutching him by the ankle.

"Where do you think you're going?" Niko yells.

Eliot kicks his leg, trying to release the grip on his ankle. But Niko won't let go. He's just a few feet from the entryway and if he can get loose, he'd be able to fly through the door into the sky, high above the buildings and out of sight. But Niko's strength is twice that of Eliot and there's no way to shake him.

"Get down here, bitch," Niko yells.

Eliot continues to struggle, but he can't get the elf to let go. His wings are flapping so fiercely that he's beginning to get weak. He's not sure how long he can keep it up.

Niko holds up his knife. "If you don't come down, I'll slash your wings so that you'll never fly again."

As Niko says this, Eliot panics. He kicks at Niko's face with his free leg, smacking him on the nose with his bare foot. It causes the elf to loosen his grip on his ankle and he flies for the entryway.

But before Eliot can get very far, Niko leaps into the air and grabs him by the waist, then pulls him to the ground. The second his wings hit the floor, Niko drops his weight down on top of him. The crunch of Eliot's wings against the linoleum, folded back the wrong way beneath the elf's weight, causes him to cry out in pain. But the elf doesn't care. He puts his arm down on Eliot's chest, right between the fairy's breasts, holding him in place.

"I tried to be a nice guy," Niko tells him. "I tried to make it easy on you. But you insist on fucking with me. You shouldn't have been so stuck up."

Niko puts the knife up to Eliot's neck and then grabs one of his breasts with his free hand. The second the elf touches him, Eliot punches him with tiny fists, pushing him away, trying to get the asshole off of him.

"Your tits are so small and soft, girl," Niko says, tightening his thighs against Eliot's hips. "You feel like a teenage girl. I like it."

Eliot looks back at Oona but he only sees her lower body at his angle, her upper body blocked by the chair between them. Her tentacles whip and thrash around at the two men as they kick and punch her body. She sprays a cloud of ink at them and they squeal at the sickening black goo but it doesn't slow their assault by much.

"Leave her alone…" Eliot whines.

But he should obviously worry more about himself. Niko has him pinned to the ground, rubbing his naked flesh with his free hand. Eliot doesn't know what he should do. His only defense is too dangerous for him to release voluntarily. Maybe if he wasn't in the same room as Oona…

"That's nice," Niko says, leaning in closer. "I like you. You're my pretty little butterfly."

Eliot is so much lighter and smaller than the elf that there's not much he can do. He almost wants the elf to cut his throat, just finish it so that he doesn't have to endure what the man wants to do to him. Eliot doesn't want to die but he does kind of like the idea of taking the elf with him. The only reason he doesn't act on the impulse is because he's worried about Oona. He doesn't know what will happen to her if he just gives up and dies. He has to hold out as long as he can.

Oona cries out. Eliot can't tell what is happening, but he sees purple blood pooling on the floor beneath her, mixing with the black ink. Even though she's the one that's crying, it seems that the elves are the ones getting more roughed up in the scuffle. Eliot can only see their legs, but they are repeatedly being knocked back and hitting the ground, as Oona's tentacles whip around like angry snakes.

Niko leans in and smells Eliot's neck. Although Eliot has never noticed it himself, everyone says that he smells like flowers. It's a natural scent that all fairies discharge when they feel scared or excited. But each fairy smells like a different kind of flower, depending on their genes.

As Niko inhales deeper, he says, "Tulips. You smell like tulips."

Eliot once had a girlfriend who said he smelled like violets, but most people say he smells like tulips as Niko identified. To Eliot he just smells normal so he can't tell one way or another. As Niko lays down on him, drawing in the scent, he smiles at the pleasant odor and then kisses Eliot's naked shoulder.

"You're a dream, do you know that?" Niko tells him. "You should be my girlfriend. I would treat you like a princess every day of your life."

Eliot wants to scream but no sound is coming out of his mouth. There's nothing worse than when people treat him as a woman. Even when he's in female form, he's a man. That's what he identifies as. He's not into men even when his body is that of a woman's. The last thing he ever wants to be is somebody's girlfriend, somebody's princess. If Niko keeps going Eliot will scratch his eyes out with his inch-long glittery fingernails.

As Niko pinches Eliot's swelling pink nipple, he says, "You like that, don't you? I know you want me. You might be trying to resist but your body doesn't lie. It wants nothing more than elf dick riding you until your wings cover me in your glitter."

Eliot is horrified by his words. There's nothing about the gross man that Eliot finds attractive. And the idea that fairies spray glitter when they orgasm is a complete myth. The glitter-like substance that they release is just a collection of dead skin cells from their fairy wings, hair and fingernails that shed at random. It's not a sexual thing. It is more likely caused by dehydration.

"Get off of me," Eliot cries.

But Niko doesn't listen to him. "Just let me fuck you. Everything will be better if you stop resisting and give into your body's urges."

The elf caresses Eliot's cheek with one hand, but presses the knife tighter to his throat. The drunken look in his eyes says that he's not going to give up until he gets what he wants. There's a part of Eliot that thinks it might be easier to just get it over with, let him do whatever he wants to his body until he's done and loses interest, but there's something in him that refuses to give in. There's still fight in him that pulls his head away from the elf's hand that pushes against his body, despite the knife pushing tighter against his throat.

"I like it when you resist," Niko says. "You're going to be a perfect birthday fuck."

As Niko puts his hand between Eliot's legs, rubbing his vagina to get it wet, Eliot freaks out. He lifts himself up, pushing the elf away from him, not giving a shit if the knife cuts him. When the elf puts a finger inside, Eliot punches him in the face as hard as he can.

The elf just laughs. The punch doesn't even spread the blood on his already-bloodied eye. He takes off his suit coat with one hand, then pulls down his pants, all while holding the knife to Eliot's neck.

Even if Oona could see what was going on, there's nothing that she could do to help. She's still fighting off the other two elves despite having guns pointed at her head. They could kill her at any second if they wanted to, but something is holding them back. Maybe it's because they don't kill unless on command or maybe because Oona has already disarmed them and it has devolved into a fist fight. Either way, Eliot knows the struggle still continues and there's nothing he can do to help it.

"You'd like me as a boyfriend," Niko says, his voice in a sexual whisper as his face moves toward Eliot's crotch, speaking to his vulva as though he's planning to suck him off. "I'm an important man. Any woman would love to have me as a boyfriend."

The second Niko kisses his bald pubic region, just above his labia, Eliot finds an opportunity to escape. Because the elf's weight is no longer pinning him down, Eliot's able to kick the asshole in the face and push off into the air.

Before the elf's lips reach his vagina, Eliot gets two feet off the ground, his wings flapping in fury, trying to make a dash for the exit.

Niko grabs his lower half and yells, "Where do you think you're going?"

Eliot kicks his little legs, but the elf won't let go. The upper part of his body lifts into the air as his wings flitter madly. Niko gets annoyed and grabs him by the waist and throws him back to the ground. He drops his pants to his ankles and lunges at Eliot.

Before the elf's penis can touch him, Eliot reaches toward Niko and grabs him by the testicles. He doesn't even realize what he's doing until he has one in his hand, trying to pop it like a kiwi.

"Let go, you bitch!" Niko screams.

But Eliot won't let go. He keeps squeezing. Then he tugs, trying to rip it off.

The elf loses interest in fucking Eliot and his attraction turns to wrath. He stabs at Eliot's wrist, trying to stop him from grabbing him in such a way. As the knife cuts into Eliot's veins, the fairy lets go, recoiling in pain.

Once his testicle is released, Niko looks at Eliot and cries, "I just wanted to love you. Now I'm going to have to kill you."

But before Niko can cut him again, Eliot shows him the wound on his wrist. The elf cut a vein in Eliot's wrist so deeply that his silver blood is gushing out. It flows onto the fairy's belly in a thick soup. The blood quivers and squirms as it pours out, moving like a living orgasm.

When Niko sees the blood moving in such a strange way, he pauses and pulls back.

"Wait a minute..." the elf says, pointing at the blood. "Is that—"

But before he can finish, the blood transforms into three razor-sharp blades that stab into his neck, chest and face. Eliot just watches the panic in the elf's eyes as the liquid metal blood twists in a spiral and cuts Niko's head from his shoulders.

CHAPTER
THREE

Niko's body goes limp and his head drops from his shoulders, landing in the fairy's lap. Eliot whimpers as gore oozes from the elf's lips, soaking his inner thighs. He thrusts his hips to knock the severed head to the floor, unable to look away from the lifeless stare in the dead man's eyes. But the silver blood isn't finished with the rapist. It transforms into a blender and slashes the man's corpse into even smaller pieces, splattering him across the walls.

Eliot grabs his wrist, trying to hold his blood inside, but so much has escaped that there's not much he can do at this point. The other elves see their leader in pieces and cry out. Bronze Hair's screams are cut short as the blood shoots across the room and pierces into his skull. His mouth drops open and his gun falls to the ground. He dies before he hits the ground.

Oona's eyes meet Eliot's and he tells her, "Get away! I can't control it!"

The octomaid jumps to the ground, squeezing under the tattoo chair, just as the blood moves in her direction. It slices into the remaining elf, cutting him open. The metallic blood becomes seven sword-like blades and slashes open Silver Hair's torso as he fires his gun in the air. He cries out only once, looking at his fallen friends briefly before he dies.

The blood just hovers in the air, looking for more prey. When it senses Oona hiding under the tattoo chair, it spreads out into a dozen long metal spikes, ready to drive itself into her body. But Eliot grabs the stream of silver blood and pulls on it, forcing it back into his wrist. The blood resists him at first, desperate to impale the octomaid as it did the elves, but Eliot won't let it have its way. He continues to tug on the silver stream until it gives in and retracts into his body.

When all the blood has returned to his veins, Eliot grips his wrist as tightly as he can, trying to stop the bleeding. He looks around at the dead bodies. His blood has never killed so many before. He never even knew it was possible.

Oona crawls out from under the tattoo chair and looks around. The room is covered in elf blood. She raises herself up and looks down at Eliot with enraged eyes. At first, he thought she would be happy that he saved them, but she's obviously far from pleased.

"You have sentient blood," Oona says to him. "Why didn't you tell me?"

Eliot holds his wrist tight and flutters himself to his feet. His breasts flatten on his chest as he transforms back into a man.

"It's normally no big deal," he says, holding his hands over his pubic region as his penis grows into his palms.

Oona slithers through the dead elves to get closer to Eliot.

She says, "I tattoo you every week. This is the kind of information I should know about."

Eliot wipes the elf blood from his crotch with a washcloth, flutters the gore out of his wings like a honey bee after getting submerged in a swimming pool. "It's not dangerous if you don't cut a major blood vessel. The amount of blood released when you tattoo me can't do any harm."

Oona just looks him in the eyes and shakes her head.

"Still…" she says. "You should have told me. It's dangerous. You could have killed me."

Eliot frowns at her and droops his wings, looking like a little lost puppy dog. Then he recovers his clothes and tries to put them on while still putting pressure on his wound.

"I'm sorry…" he says. "I thought you wouldn't tattoo me if you knew."

Oona looks away, trying to brush off the betrayal. She points at the dead bodies and says, "You shouldn't have done that. These guys are dangerous."

Eliot looks at the dead elves. Even though the room is covered in body parts, he can't help but smile.

"They're not dangerous anymore," he says.

Oona blinks at his words. "They're far more dangerous dead than alive. Niko is the son of Shino Kaji, boss of the Kaji family. If he finds out what you did to his son he won't only kill you, he'll kill every member of your family and everyone you've ever loved."

Eliot looks down at the pieces of elf. "I've never heard of the Kaji family."

"You've heard of the Sylphs, right?" Oona asks. "The elf yakuza. They run everything around here."

When Eliot hears the word *Sylph*, he knows exactly what she's talking about. They are the main people responsible for trafficking fairykind. They are the most dangerous group in the city. Eliot is finally beginning to understand the severity of their situation.

"Nobody can know we did this," Oona says. "We have to get rid of the bodies. Destroy all the evidence."

"How do we do that?" Eliot asks.

Oona looks down, trying to come up with a plan. They stand there in silence for a few minutes. Eliot tries to think of a plan as well. He finishes putting on his clothes, lacing up his combat boots when an idea hits him.

"What if we got help from somebody in the Snake Pit?"

Eliot asks. "Your boss is Madam Nuri, right? Maybe she can fix this."

Oona shakes her head. "Madam Nuri's the last person who can know. She'll do anything it takes to keep peace with the Kaji and won't hesitate handing over our heads if she thinks it will help. She's spent her whole life building bridges with the other three families. The Sylphs, the Naiads, the Dyrads... Madam Nuri has business ties with all of them. She's the queen of the fire races in the underworld and believes that fire is strongest when combined with other elements. Wood growing from the earth is fuel for a fire. Air is necessary for fire to breathe and the wind helps it spread. Water can help prevent fire from burning out of control. While all the other families are at war with each other, only the fire family is the one that stays neutral, gaining in strength and resources. It's Madam Nuri's philosophy that has helped us flourish for the past six decades. Right now, she's our biggest threat. If she finds out, we're finished."

"What if we got help from someone else, though?" Eliot asks. "I'm friends with Tiki and Taka who work in the club. They might be employed by Madam Nuri, but they're just strippers. They aren't fire family. I know they'll help. Lamias can swallow people whole."

Oona shakes her head. "We can't risk it. The more people who know, the more likely Madam Nuri will find out."

Eliot pleads with her. "But I trust them. They're like my sisters. They can get rid of the bodies for us."

He's seen them do it before. He walked in on them once, in one of the back rooms of the strip club. They service clients with a sexual fetish for being swallowed alive by lamias. Although real snakes can swallow prey by unhinging their jaws, lamias swallow prey in a different way. Their vaginas are connected to their digestive tracts and are extremely flexible. Back in ancient times, before the civilized world was formed, lamias used to prey on humans and other humanoid races. They'd seduce them, inject them with poison or constrict them with their tails in order to immobilize them, and then pull them into their bodies.

These days, lamias only feed this way on request. It costs around a thousand dollars to be partially swallowed for a few minutes and then spit back out. For fifty thousand dollars, a lamia will completely devour a man. This is what Eliot witnessed when he caught the snake twins by surprise one day. He saw just the head of a guy sticking out of Tiki's lower mouth as he licked her clitoris. Taka was lying next to her with a man-shaped bulge in the snake half of her body, having already completely swallowed her customer just moments earlier.

They told Eliot to meet them back there at that time, but they must have forgotten to watch the clock or maybe they forgot he was coming all together. It's also possible that they wanted him to walk in on them. They never missed an opportunity to embarrass him. They always loved to see him blush.

When Eliot pulled open the curtain, he was shocked to see Tiki moaning and writhing, grinding the man's head into her outstretched labia, her reptilian hand tightly gripping the back of his neck. The moment she saw Eliot in the entryway, a mischievous look spread across her face, like she was a kid being caught with her hand in a cookie jar.

"Oh, Eliot!" she cried, smiling. Then she quickly slurped the rest of the man up, gulping him in an instant, as though trying to hide the evidence. "You came!"

Her vagina sealed tightly behind her customer's head, constricting firmly to keep her prey from trying to get back out the way he went in, no longer visible between her red snake scales.

"We're on lunch break," Taka said, clearing a space on the

bench between them. "Come sit with us!"

The red racer twins seemed to just brush it all off as no big deal, just another day at work, but Eliot was in too much shock to just sit down and ignore what happened. When they realized his awkwardness, they explained everything. They said one of the biggest sources of revenue for the Snake Pit was serving customers with strange fetishes like this one. Eliot couldn't believe there were people who actually paid to be eaten by them. It sounded like a horrific way to die.

"Most of our clients are suicidal or have fatal diseases," Tiki told him. "They want to die in a sexy way rather than in a hospital or by cutting their wrists."

"But not these guys," Taka said, patting the bulge in her scales. "They were just drunk and horny."

Tiki added, "They've been regulars for the past few years and finally had the money and courage to go all the way."

Taka laughed. "It also helped that we kept giving them free drinks all night."

Tiki giggled with her. "Yeah, it took quite a while to convince them. I can't believe they actually went for it."

Eliot still couldn't believe it. He had no idea his friends did this on a regular basis. The girls put their tops back on and Eliot sat down on the bench next to Tiki, close to the door. He wasn't sure he could trust them after watching them kill these men. Even though they were his friends, he was worried they might want to eat him for dessert. He's small enough that they probably would still have room for a little fairy.

"We wanted you to hang out with us while we're digesting," Taka explained to him. "We're not allowed to leave the room until we're ready to poop them out."

Tiki groaned, gripping her bulge. "It's the most boring part of the job. We want you to keep us company."

"Why can't you leave the room?" Eliot asked.

"Because it's illegal to eat people, silly." Tiki giggled at him as though it was a stupid question to ask. "As long as nobody sees our swollen stomachs there's no proof that it ever happened."

"Yeah, once we shit them out there's no evidence that it ever happened," Taka said. "There's no corpse to find. Even their bones get digested."

Eliot cringed at the thought. He looked down at the man-shaped lumps in their bodies. The poor saps must have already been dead at that point. The twins' lower halves pulsed and squeezed, compressing the men into tight little balls, pushing them deeper into their digestive systems, crushing them like mice inside a boa constrictor. It seemed so brutal, yet both of the men paid to have this happen to them. Eliot would never choose to die in such a way.

"You're our alibi," Taka told Eliot. "If anyone asks, tell them we were giving you a lap dance this whole time."

"How long will it take?" Eliot asked.

Tiki responded, "We took some pills to speed up the process, so they'll go through our systems pretty quickly. Maybe three hours."

"That's a long lap dance," Eliot said.

"Well, you're a special customer," Tiki said, curling up close to Eliot. "We always give our best customers extra attention."

Eliot was surprised to hear this. "I'm not really a customer, though. I'm just a friend."

"Nobody has to know that." Taka slithered to the other side of the bench next to him.

"So what do we do for the next three hours?" Eliot asked.

"Just cuddle with us," Tiki said, hugging his arm and nuzzling her head into his shoulder. "It feels good to cuddle while digesting prey."

Then Taka laid her head in his lap and pulled his free hand to her coiled tail.

"Pet my scales," she said.

Eliot reluctantly complied. It was the most awkward experience he'd ever had with the twins, but he did as they asked. He was their friend, after all. Eliot didn't have many friends, so he made sure to do whatever they wanted, even if it meant becoming an accomplice to a very serious crime.

He never realized it was so easy for lamias to get away with murder. He knew that if he ever needed somebody dead or if he ever needed to get rid of a body, they would be the ones to call.

After Eliot explains how useful the lamia twins could be to get rid of the elf bodies, Oona goes quiet and thinks about it for a minute.

"It's perfect," Eliot says. "Their bodies would never be found. Nobody would connect us to their deaths."

Oona stares him in the eyes. "Are you sure we can trust them? If they go straight to Madam Nuri the second we explain this to them we'd be fucked."

Eliot says, "I don't think they know these guys are important. They just saw Niko as a creepy asshole that kept harassing everyone in the club. They seemed to hate him. I bet they'd be happy to get rid of the bodies for us."

Oona lets out a sigh and says, "It's not a bad plan. Maybe it would work."

"I'm sure it would work," Eliot says. "Should I go get them?"

Oona pauses for a minute, thinking it over.

"Nevermind," she says. "It's not a good plan."

Eliot can't believe it. "What do you mean? It's perfect."

She shakes her head. "Even if we can get rid of the evidence, everyone knows that Niko was last seen at the Snake Pit. Shino Kaji would hold Madam Nuri responsible. Eventually they'd figure out what happened."

Eliot sits down and rubs the antennae on his forehead. He knows she's right. Besides, now that he thinks about it, he doesn't like the idea of bringing Tiki and Taka into this. He doesn't want to cause them trouble. They might not even want to be his friend anymore if he took advantage of their friendship like that.

"Then what should we do?" Eliot asks.

"We have to pin it on the Naiads somehow," Oona says. "Everyone will buy that. The Naiads and Sylphs are in a blood feud right now. Shino Kaji and his son are both prime targets for Naiad hitmen. It would make perfect sense if Niko was targeted tonight, on the day of his promotion."

"Wait…" Eliot says, confused by her suggestion. "Why would you want to blame it on the Naiads? Aren't they *your* people?"

Oona narrows her eyes at him. "The Naiads aren't my people."

"But you're an octomaid," Eliot says. "I thought…"

"Just because I'm an octomaid that doesn't mean I have any ties to the mermaid mafia," she says. "I hate the Naiads more than anyone, even more than the Sylphs. I'd gladly pin this on those assholes. I hope it gets a lot of them killed."

Eliot nods, not wanting to pry any further. It sounds like Oona knows what she's talking about, so Eliot decides to agree with going in this direction, even though feeding the body parts to lamias would have been the quickest and easiest way to solve the problem.

"So, how do we make people believe it was the Naiads?" he asks.

Oona squints and gives it a thought. "We need to get the bodies to Naiad territory. Make it look like a hit."

Eliot looks at the corpses. "But they don't look like they were shot. They're in pieces."

"A lot of Naiad assassins, especially those of the shark men race, tear their victims limb from limb. Even if there aren't any teeth marks, it will be believable enough. These guys must have been hopping strip clubs, so we should find a mermaid strip club in Naiad territory. Park their car in the parking lot and drop their corpses in a back alley. It shouldn't be too difficult. I think it will work."

"But won't people be suspicious if they never actually entered the strip club?"

Oona shakes her head. "It doesn't matter. As long as they are found in Naiad territory, Shino Kaji will blame it on the mermaids. We just need to get there without anyone spotting us. We also need to figure out which vehicle Niko came in. Hopefully he didn't take a cab."

Eliot lets out a sigh, then nods his head. "Okay. We can do this. Where do we start?"

Oona points at the floor. "We clean this place up."

It takes a couple hours, but eventually the tattoo shop is so clean that nobody would have suspected three murders took place here. The three bodies are wrapped in garbage bags. The floor is sparkling clean. There are no signs of a struggle.

Oona holds out three pairs of keys. "You have to find their car."

When Eliot takes the keys, he looks down at them, confused about what she's asking. "Did they come in three cars or just one?"

Oona shrugs. "Hopefully they all came in one. If they arrived separately it will be difficult to take multiple trips without raising suspicion." She points at one set of keys with a steel cat head keychain. "These are Niko's keys. Focus on finding out which car these belong to. As long as Niko's car leaves the area we should be fine."

Eliot nods. He hopes they don't have to move more than one vehicle. He doesn't want this to be any more complicated than it already is.

"Do you know how to drive?" she asks.

"Yeah, but I haven't driven since moving to the city. I don't have a driver's license."

"It's fine. We're fucked if we get pulled over anyway so you don't need a license. I want you to go find the car and pull it into the back alley so we can load the bodies into the trunk. Don't let anyone see you. If anyone witnesses you getting into Niko's car we'll be screwed."

Eliot nods and goes to his backpack. "I'll wear my hoodie so I don't attract too much attention."

It's what immediately comes to his mind. If his wings are showing everyone will be looking at him. It's difficult to be incognito when you're a fairy. But if people think he's just an ordinary street kid, people won't even look in his direction.

"Just be as quick as you can," Oona says, packing her tattoo equipment into a large purse.

Eliot leaves the tattoo shop, his wings hidden under his hoodie, the wound on his wrist covered in tattoo bandages. He enters the strip club bustling with lights and music and a crowd that has doubled in size from earlier. He pulls up his hood to cover his antennae and hair, trying to blend in. Nobody looks at him as he enters the crowd, he'd rather hide from even the bouncers. He doesn't want anyone to know he left the club the same time Niko's car disappears from the parking lot.

But before he gets too far, somebody calls out to him, "Hey, Eliot!"

He turns around to see Tiki slithering toward him.

"Forgetting something?" she asks.

Eliot doesn't want to talk to anyone right now, not even his friends. But he has no choice but to wait for her to come to him. He doesn't want to act suspiciously, even though he's so nervous that anyone would be able to pick up on it if they were paying attention.

Tiki holds up Eliot's skateboard. "You left this at the bar."

When he sees the board in her hand, Eliot exhales a sigh of relief. He had no idea he had forgotten his skateboard. He must have been so unnerved when Niko hit on him earlier that he forgot all about it.

"Thanks," Eliot says, as he takes the skateboard from her and weaves it between the straps of his backpack.

"No problem," Tiki says. "How did your tattoo session go?"

"Okay…" he says, standing in the middle of a crowd facing the dance stage.

"Is it a good one?" she asks. "Can I see it?"

Before he has a chance to respond, Taka comes up behind him and wraps her arms around his back.

"Of course it's great," Taka says. "All of Oona's tattoos are amazing."

Before they can pull up Eliot's shirt, he holds his hoodie down tightly and says, "I'll show you when it's healed. It doesn't look good right now."

He doesn't want them to see it because the tattoo isn't finished. He's worried that they would think it was weird if they saw that Oona didn't finish it yet, because she's known to never stop until she's done. Even on big projects she'll work for fifteen hours straight until she's satisfied with the final product. They might know something's wrong if she didn't complete such a simple tattoo.

"But you always show us your tattoos," Tiki says.

Eliot shakes his head. "Not this time."

They frown at him but don't push any further.

"Did you also get tattooed on your wrist?" Taka asks, pointing at the bandage sticking out of his hoodie sleeve.

When Eliot notices the bandage showing, he pulls down his sleeve and says, "Umm… yeah, she touched up an older tattoo."

They just look at him, not sure what he's talking about.

Tiki changes the subject. "Hey, you know that creepy guy that was hitting on you earlier?"

Eliot freezes up when she says this. He wonders if she knows anything.

"Yeah…" he says.

"You haven't seen him anywhere, have you?" Tiki says. "He disappeared without paying his bar tab. Nikki is pissed."

"Nikki?" Eliot asks.

Eliot's breath becomes heavy. He doesn't know how he should respond.

"We thought he might have gone after you once we left you alone," Taka says. "Somebody said they saw him follow you out back."

Eliot's heart pounds. He's afraid it might already be over; he's already been caught. If the last time anyone saw Niko was chasing down Eliot, it won't be long before people connect the dots.

He doesn't know what to say but, "No, I didn't see him again after he talked to me at the bar."

The snake twins just shrug.

"Huh… that's strange," Tiki says. "Guess he must have just been sneaking out the back door."

"What a scumbag," Taka says. "He acted like he was all rich and important and then ran out on his bill."

Eliot tries to brush it off. "Maybe he just forgot to pay."

"Whatever…" Tiki says. Then she changes the subject. "So are you leaving now or do you want to have another drink with us?"

Eliot is already inching away from them, trying to get out of the conversation as quickly as possible.

"I'm sorry…" he says. "I've got stuff to do."

"Aww…" Taka grabs his arm and curls her tail around his legs. "Stay with us. It's going to be boring without you."

Tiki puts on her cutest puppy dog face. "We promised to give you a lap dance."

Eliot just shakes his head and pulls himself out of Taka's grip. "I can't. Maybe next time."

As he walks away from them, they just say, "Boo…"

But he keeps on walking. He doesn't even say goodbye as he pushes himself through the crowd toward the exit.

Outside, the street is lined with cars and people walking up and down the sidewalks. He has no idea how he's going to be able to find Niko's car. It could be any of them. There's also a chance that Niko's car might have a driver or bodyguard or somebody he works with that he left behind to watch his vehicle.

Eliot looks for the most expensive-looking car, thinking the son of a notorious yakuza boss has to drive something nice. Most of the cars on the block are pretty junky. The Snake Pit isn't known for the most classy clientele, so finding a fancy car shouldn't be too difficult. But as he scans the street, nothing jumps out at him.

He walks down the sidewalk, making sure no one is watching him as he goes from vehicle to vehicle. He's too intimidated to try each one, waiting until he finds the most likely option before testing the keys. But none of the cars seem like anything a rich kid would drive. After walking three blocks down, he crosses the street and tries the other side of the road. But there's nothing remotely similar to the type of car he's looking for.

Oona put him on a much more difficult task than Eliot realized. He wonders if Niko parked blocks away. He might have even found a gated parking lot somewhere to keep his car safe. Or maybe he took a cab or was dropped off by a yakuza driver. All of these possibilities would ruin their plan.

As he goes further up the block, he sees an SUV that grabs his attention. It's not that it's a particularly nice vehicle, totally not what he was expecting a yakuza would drive, but what piques his interest is that it is perfectly clean with a shiny black paint job you don't normally see on this type of automobile. It also has dark tinted windows, a shade that isn't even legal in this state. It's worth a try.

He's across the street, but still within view of the bouncers at the door of the Snake Pit. There's also a line of customers waiting to get in. Eliot stays on the passenger side of the vehicle, trying to keep out of view. Luckily he's so short that nobody can see him over the tall roof of the SUV.

But just when he thinks he lucked out, he realizes that Niko's key doesn't work. It's not his vehicle. He looks farther up the road, wondering if there might be another car that might be a reasonable choice, but he doesn't see anything.

"Damn it to hell," Eliot says.

He decides to try another key from the keychain. It would make more sense if this SUV belonged to one of Niko's friends. The yakuza boss's son wouldn't drive such an unflashy vehicle, but maybe one of his underlings would. He tries both sets of keys. None of them work.

"Shit…"

But just before he gives up, Eliot notices the license plate of the car in front of the SUV. The plate reads *NEKOPARA*. Above the plate is a picture of a cat head identical to the one on Niko's keychain. Nekopara is an erotic Japanese cartoon that means *Cat Paradise*. It's a cliché that Japanese elves are into neko girls, the race of cat-like people that are considered a subspecies on that side of the world. Eliot has never met one in person, but they are supposed to be as popular as fairies among the elven race. Nekos tend to be kept as pets for rich elven families, usually serving as cooks or housekeepers when they aren't entertaining the family children.

Eliot steps closer to the vehicle. It's a junky old car with a chipped up paint job, but it's actually not the kind of thing that somebody of the lower class would drive. It's a classic Mercedes Benz from the early '60s. Even in rough shape, this car would be worth quite a lot.

The key fits in the door. It's definitely Niko's. Perhaps the car was a recent purchase and hasn't been fixed up yet or maybe it has sentimental value and the Kaji brat likes it just the way it is. Either way, Eliot takes a breath of relief the second the door unlocks.

Eliot takes a few looks around before he gets inside the car. A few people see him get in, but they're not paying enough attention to think anything's wrong with the scenario. He's almost fully relaxed until he gets in the driver's seat and realizes that the car doesn't have automatic transmission. He's never driven stick before. He has no idea how he's going to get it into the back alley.

He puts the car into first and drives two feet before it stalls out. Everyone outside of the club looks over at him. He starts it back up drives out of the spot, keeping it in first gear the whole way around the corner and into the back alleyway, the engine roaring with every meter it moves. There's not a person who doesn't notice the vehicle as it chugs around the back of the building. Luckily, none of them seem like anyone of consequence. Nobody who works at the Snake Pit notice. Nobody who would have any ties to the Kaji or Nuri families.

When he pulls up out front of the back exit to the tattoo shop, Oona is glaring at him like he's the biggest idiot in the world, like she made a huge mistake in trusting him with the job of getting the vehicle. All of the garbage bags are in her tentacles, one dangling over shoulder, two held at her hip. Eliot can't believe she's able to lift the weight of three elves at once. With her massive size, Eliot knew she was strong, but she's even stronger than he thought.

"You took too long," she says, the second the car stalls out and he steps out of the driver seat.

He's about to explain that he doesn't drive stick when she interrupts him to say, "Pop open the trunk."

He does what she says. There isn't anyone to see her put the garbage bags in the trunk, despite the fact that this is the place where the Snake Pit strippers tend to gather and smoke on their breaks. They have to hurry though. Someone could come out at any second.

"I'll drive the rest of the way," Oona tells him.

He moves to the passenger seat and lets her in. She doesn't hesitate to slam on the gas and roar their way out of there, moving too quickly for anyone to notice who's driving as they speed through the alleys toward the main drag.

CHAPTER
FOUR

Eliot can't help but admire how Oona operates the old Mercedes. He always assumed an octomaid would have trouble driving an automobile, but she's able to handle it even better than a bipedal person would. Her tentacles have perfect control over the stick shift and pedals, not even needing to use her hands to steer if she didn't want to. The only problem is that her tentacles are so thick and long that they spill out over her seat, squishing against Eliot's arm and flopping into his lap. They squirm around like they have minds of their own, curling up to the ceiling, dangling out the window.

The tentacles are wet and oily, as though Oona had taken a dip in her fish tank just before getting into the car. The liquid soaks through Eliot's hoodie, drenching him in salt water and fishy slime. After ten minutes of driving down the freeway, the cold air sends a chill down his sopping parts. But Eliot kind of enjoys being squished into the small vehicle with the large woman. He feels special being so close to her without having to be tattooed. He wishes he could spend more time with her like this, outside of the tattoo shop. He just wishes it would have been under different circumstances.

"So how long have you had it?" Oona asks him, breaking the silence.

Eliot has no idea what she's talking about. "Have what?"

"Your sentient blood," she says. "It's a rare disease. I've never seen it in action before."

Eliot nods. He was hoping he wouldn't have to talk about it, kind of embarrassed that Oona had to see it. Sentient blood is also known as *metal blood* or *the murder virus*. It's a sexually transmitted parasite that can only grow within the bloodstreams of sprites like fairies and pixies. Once it makes its way across the entire circulatory system it's unable to be removed without killing its host. Although it is not dangerous to those it infects, it will turn your blood hard as metal when it leaves your body and attacks anyone in the area that it views as a threat. Nothing can stop it once it's free.

"I've had it for a couple of years now," Eliot responds.

"Does it hurt?" she asks.

Eliot shakes his head. "It's no big deal."

"You got it on purpose, didn't you? For protection?"

Eliot looks over at her, then turns away and nods. "Fairies have to take drastic measures these days. You know, to stay safe."

"It's got to be a steep price to pay for safety."

Eliot nods. With sentient blood, he's not able to date anyone of fairykind anymore, not without infecting them with his parasite's offspring. Women with the parasite pass it on to their children as well, if the blood doesn't attack and kill the fetus in the womb before it is born. Most fairies won't get into a relationship with anyone with his ailment for this reason. Even non-fairies are cautious about it, terrified of what will happen to them if their lover ever accidentally cuts themselves too deeply in their presence. A fairy with sentient blood is basically a walking time bomb.

"My last girlfriend had it," Eliot tells her. "She convinced me it was a good idea to get it, so I let her infect me. We broke up a few weeks later."

"Why's that?" Oona asks.

Eliot shrugs. "Fairy girls are crazy. They suck to date. I should know, I've spent plenty of time as one."

"Oh yeah?" an odd smirk forms on her face.

"Yeah. We can be kind of emotionally… intense. We're always in your face when you want to be left alone and fly away whenever you get too close. We flip out over the littlest thing. I sometimes prefer being a woman. Female fairies have amplified senses, so I enjoy everything more as a girl. I enjoy listening to music more. I like being touched. Even food tastes better. But I get angry and depressed a lot easier, not to mention my anxiety goes through the roof. I prefer to stay a guy most of the time. It's just easier. Besides, I'm more attracted to women than men so it makes more sense to me."

Oona is quiet after that and Eliot starts to think that maybe he shouldn't have given her so much personal information. He also hopes that she isn't offended by what he said. He realizes that he might have just argued that women are more crazy and emotionally unstable compared to men, which she obviously might not like to hear, but he just meant that about fairies. Because his kind are so gender fluid, sexism isn't really an issue among them. They openly talk about what they like and don't like about being male versus female. Talking about your gender preferences is about as casual as arguing about what style of shoes you prefer.

After a moment of silence, Oona focusing more on driving than their conversation, she eventually speaks up and asks, "Have you ever killed anyone with your blood before?"

Eliot pauses. He wasn't expecting the conversation to take such a dark path. He thinks about it for a moment but decides to come clean.

"Yeah," he says. "Once."

"What happened?"

"It was similar to what happened today," Eliot says. "A guy wanted to have sex with me at knife point. He threatened to cut me and I let him. I left him bleeding to death in the bathroom of a bar."

"So you're able to handle all this?" Oona asks.

Eliot nods. "Rapists deserve what's coming to them."

They take an exit off the freeway and enter the Naiad side of town. Eliot hasn't really visited this area before. Very few people come here unless they have to. Nobody likes the mermaid ghetto, not even the people who live here.

This side of town is different from the rest of the city. It's like entering a different country, set up to accommodate merfolk rather than bipeds. There are more canals than streets, more lakes than parks. Even buildings are supposed to be mostly underwater. It's not a place built for fairykind. Eliot can feel his anxiety building the second they leave the freeway.

As they drive beside a canal, Eliot can see all the merfolk swimming alongside them. There are dolphin and shark fins, sea serpent people and even those of the walrus and manatee race. They pass a group of mermaids sitting on the side of the canal outside the water, covered in cheap tattoos and piercings, smoking black weed cigarettes and drinking some kind of alcoholic sludge out of mason jars probably made from kelp or algae. They are barely dressed, wearing fishnet tank tops or spiked leather bikinis. Some of them don't wear any clothes at all, bathing their naked fish scales in the moonlight. Every neighborhood has its street trash, but Eliot's never seen mermaid gutter punks before. They seem twice as intimidating as the punks in his neighborhood. He would never be caught dead swimming in that canal with all of them around. They'd probably drown him the second they saw him.

Mermaids were once considered one of the most beautiful races, almost equal to fairies. But it's been decades since they've been viewed as anything but gutter scum. Visually they are enchanting, but the quality of merfolk neighborhoods has deteriorated over the years. Their waterways are full of sewage and pollution causing their scales to lose their colorful beauty. People tend to be prejudiced against merfolk, assuming they all smell of raw sewage and rotten fish. This is usually the case, but it's not their fault. If the city gave them cleaner waterways to live in, if there were more jobs that accommodated their kind, if people treated them with more respect, maybe they would be able to return to their former glory.

"I know of a place that will be perfect to drop the bodies," Oona says. "But it's not very safe. Definitely not for you."

"They don't like fairies?" Eliot asks.

"They don't like anyone on two legs," Oona says. "You'll probably be okay if you act like a customer ready to toss down a ton of money. But people won't like you in this neighborhood. If they find out you're a fairy they'll rip you apart."

"Why?" Eliot asks, his anxiety rising to an even higher level.

"Mermaids are very competitive. They'll see a fairy as a threat, especially the dancers at the club. There's a lot of pent up aggression in this neighborhood so they're just looking to find someone to take it out on. You don't want to expose your wings for a second."

"Are we going in?" Eliot asks. "I thought we were just dropping off the bodies in an alley behind the club."

"I have a friend who works there who will help us out. She hates the Naiads as much as I do and would love to help escalate their war with the Sylphs. She'll get us out of here without raising suspicion and make sure Niko's death isn't blamed on us."

When Eliot hears this, he can't believe his ears. "I thought you said you didn't want anyone else involved. That's why you wouldn't let me get help from Tiki and Taka."

Oona shakes her head. "This is different. Avia is like a sister to me and she would sooner die than give me up."

Eliot frowns, but decides not to be too upset. He trusts Oona knows what she's doing. If she says her friend will help, he believes her. He just wishes she trusted his friends as much as he's expected to trust hers.

They pull up to a large dark building far from the freeway, deep into Naiad territory. The place doesn't have any neon signs out front. There's no windows. No lights in the parking lot whatsoever. It'll be perfect for them to ditch the car without being seen, but it doesn't seem very safe wandering in the dark in such a dangerous neighborhood. Without even seeing the inside, Eliot can tell the place is shady as hell. He thought the Snake Pit was bad, but this place takes seedy strip club to a whole new level.

"Are you sure this is even a strip club?" Eliot asks. "It looks more like an opium den."

Oona nods her head. "It's a mermaid brothel, actually. The Naiad family owns it. If Niko was dumb enough to come here to get laid he would have been killed for sure. It'll be perfect."

"Who's going to believe he was dumb enough to come here then?"

"Everyone knows he's that dumb," Oona says. "It's just the kind of thing he'd do."

They try to act as casual as possible as they take the bodies from the trunk and carry them behind the building. There isn't much of an alley back here. It's just a dumpster and the back entrance to the brothel. A couple cars are parked back here. It doesn't seem like the kind of place they were looking for.

Once they drop the bags, Eliot starts to feel uncomfortable with their plan. It doesn't seem like it will work.

"Are you sure we should leave them here?" Eliot asks.

Oona nods. "It's as good a place as any."

Eliot scratches his neck. "I mean… If people from the club killed the elves back here, why would they just leave the bodies right on their doorstep where anyone could find them? You'd think they'd try to get rid of the bodies as soon as they did the deed."

"That's the beauty of it," Oona says. "The first people to find the bodies will be the Naiad family. They won't call the cops. They'll try to dispose of the bodies themselves, but by then there will already be plenty of witnesses. Word will get back to Shino Kaji. The second these bodies are found the Naiad will take the blame. Nobody will care that they didn't do it."

Oona cuts open the bags with her long talon-like fingernails and spills the contents all over the pavement. She scatters the blood and body parts. Then tosses the empty bags into the dumpster.

"Won't the Naiads want to know who did this, though?" Eliot asks. "They might want revenge on whoever caused them this trouble."

Oona tosses the keys and switchblade into the dumpster. "The Naiad boss put a bounty on Niko's head. He'll be happy as hell about this, probably see it as a present on his doorstep. If we brought him Niko's head in person, he would have paid us handsomely."

"Then why didn't we do that?" Eliot asks.

As they walk away from the scene, looking around to make sure no one sees them, Oona responds, "We can't let anyone know we did this. If Madame Nuri finds out, we're dead. And she would definitely find out."

They stick to the shadows as they go to the front of the building.

"Couldn't the Naiad boss be discreet? Not tell anyone?"

Oona shakes her head. "The only way he would protect us is if we joined the Naiads. And I'd rather die than work for them."

There aren't any bouncers at the door of the brothel, carding people to be let in like at the Snake Pit. Instead, there are armed guards standing inside as they step through the entrance. Two large shark men in black suits with assault rifles in their finlike arms stand at attention as they pass by. The security does not look at them or say a word. They don't need to. Just the sight of them standing there is message enough that they better not start any shit, or they're fucked.

As they go through a hallway toward the main area of the brothel, they pass all manner of clientele. Humans, centaurs, even an old cave troll crouched down to fit inside of the hall. Oona keeps her face down, staying behind Eliot as she pushes him forward, forcing him to lead the way.

"I don't want anyone to recognize me here," Oona tells Eliot, even though he never asked. "I look a lot different than the last time I visited, but I'm well known among these people. I used to live here."

"You mean you were a prostitute here?" Eliot asks.

Oona shoves him, offended that he'd even suggest such a thing.

"I lived on one of the upper floors. I would never sell my body for the Naiads."

When they step into the main room, Eliot can't believe his eyes. There's a luxurious indoor pool designed to look like a Hawaiian lagoon with fake rocks and palm trees, white sand beaches and waterfalls. Dozens of the most beautiful mermaids Eliot's ever seen are swimming in the lagoon or perched on rocks, singing entrancing siren songs in their mermaid tongue. There are also octomaids, sharkmaids, starfish girls, lobster girls, and all varieties of merfolk. They are completely different from the sewer maidens Eliot saw on the drive over. They have bright blue or green hair and makeup, wearing elegant gowns and pearl jewelry. Eliot had no idea that there still existed mermaids that were so gorgeous.

A water nymph carrying a tray of blue cocktails approaches Eliot. She's dressed in a short white skirt and halter top, platinum blonde hair, glittery blue skin with gills on her neck. A long glowing lobe like that of an anglerfish protrudes from her forehead and dangles in front of her face. She hands Eliot a cocktail that bubbles and foams, sugar coated rim, a pink umbrella on top.

"Welcome to Siren's Cove," the nymph says with a big blue smile, brushing the radiant bulb from her eyes as she would a stray lock of hair.

Then she moves on.

Eliot looks at the drink in his hand. It smells sweet yet fishy. Strips of kelp float on top of the fizzy suds.

"Don't drink it," Oona tells him. "It's laced with a powerful aphrodisiac. With your metabolism, I won't be able to pry you off of the mermaids if you take even a sip."

Eliot nods his head and lowers his glass. He really didn't have any interest in drinking it anyway.

Once they're deep into the crowd of customers, Oona breaks away from him.

"Okay, I'm going to go find Avia," she says. "Wait here and act like a customer. Don't show your wings and don't drink anything and you should be fine."

Eliot nods as she slithers away from him.

"And stay away from the mermaids," she says. "They are masters of seduction. We're not here to get you laid."

She doesn't have to tell him twice. As she leaves a trail of slime across the marble floor, Eliot watches her disappear into the crowd. Even though he's surrounded by beautiful mermaids, none of them capture his eyes as much as Oona. She's still the most beautiful woman he's ever met. As a fairy, he's always had his choice of women of any race, but Oona's the most perfect of anyone he's met. It's the first time he's ever longed for a woman, wishing she would be interested in him. Perhaps this is why he finds her so attractive. Perhaps he wants a woman who doesn't care that he's a fairy, who falls in love with him despite the beautiful wings on his back. But so far, she's not shown any interest in him, not because of his wings, not because of the person he is inside. He hopes this will change one day. He hopes this whole experience will bring them closer together.

Eliot isn't sure what he should do while waiting for Oona to come back. He sees an empty bench near the lagoon and decides to go sit down. Oona told him not to talk to the mermaids, but he assumes it's not a problem to sit and watch them from a distance. He's never seen anything like this before. It's almost like a water ballet. Mermaids sing a beautiful hymn on the big synthetic rocks while the others swim in formation around them.

Lining the walls behind the lagoon, there's an aquarium filled with even more mermaids feeding on live eels in an almost erotic display. The mermaids behind glass appear much larger than those in the lagoon. Eliot's never seen a giant mermaid before. Merfolk of all varieties are known to grow to enormous sizes, depending on the size of the body of water they live in. Deep ocean mermaids can get up to a hundred feet long if they decide never to join the civilized world. Perhaps it's just a trick of the glass and the mermaids are actually an average size or maybe they are just some of the naturally larger varieties of merfolk, like orcamaids or great white sharkmaids, but it's a stunning sight either way. Eliot couldn't imagine how terrifying it would be to swim in that tank with them. He'd feel more like a butterfly than a fairy compared to their massive size.

While watching the deep-sea mermaids, he wonders if he would still be interested in Oona if she grew that large. Octomaids can grow even larger than the tank could hold. Known as krakenmaids, they are big enough to sink ships. It's possible Oona could have grown into a krakenmaid had she never left the ocean depths. She already dwarfs Eliot in size as it is, but he imagines that he wouldn't feel any different about her if she were a kraken as long as she was still able to tattoo him. But the possibility of them dating would seem even less likely. He would be a mere insect compared to her.

As Eliot stares at the giant women in the tank, his mind

wandering, he doesn't notice the mermaid jump out of the water and slide up the tiled floor toward him. She splashes him, soaking his clothes as she leaps up onto the bench next to him, forcing Eliot to pay attention to her.

"Hi there, handsome," she says to him. "Mind if I sit next to you?"

Although Oona told him not to talk to the mermaids, he thinks it wouldn't be a good idea to refuse her. He's supposed to be an interested customer, so turning her away might be suspicious, not to mention rude.

"Sure…" he says.

The mermaid is half tropical fish, so she's very colorful with yellow and pink striped scales, fluffy spiny fins that look almost like pompoms growing out of her sides. She's more like a peacock than a fish. Eliot's never seen a mermaid like her outside of pictures. They are the kind that rich people hire to swim in aquariums at their fancy dinner parties, the kind that you don't normally get to sit and talk with. He can't believe such a rare species would work in a place like this.

She smiles with bright orange lips. "I saw you sitting here all by yourself and thought you might need some company."

Eliot nods and can't help but smile back. "Thanks."

Her fish tail flaps against the tile floor, drawing his attention. He's never been so close to a mermaid before. He can feel his heartbeat increasing as a sweet fishy perfume floods his senses. He recognizes the purpose of the scent immediately. The mermaid is releasing pheromones at him. As a fairy, he has similar pheromones known as *fairy dust* that he releases whenever he flaps his wings, only they smell more like flowers than sugary shrimp. She rubs her body to release more pheromones, caressing the area near what Eliot imagines to be her genitals. Then she touches Eliot's face, spreading them on his cheek and neck, ensuring that he becomes aroused by her.

"My name is Lily," she tells him, then she leans against him and whispers in his ear. "I hope we can be friends."

Oona was right when she said that he should avoid talking to the mermaids. He's already becoming aroused by her. With just the simplest touch he's found himself already becoming erect.

Eliot nods at her, trying to hide his erection. "I'm Eliot."

When the mermaid looks at the cocktail in his hand, she says, "You haven't even touched your drink." She grabs his cocktail and brings it to his mouth. "Try some. It's delicious."

He shakes his head and says he doesn't drink, but she doesn't listen to him. With the straw shoved toward his lips, he has no choice but to open his mouth and take a sip.

"Yeah, it's good." he says, and takes another sip.

The drink is strong with both alcohol and other chemicals, but tastes delicious. Even with the pungent seaweed flavor, it tastes of tangy tropical fruit that dances on his tongue.

"I'm happy you like it," she says, and smiles again.

The effects of the drink hit him almost immediately. It's not like a normal alcohol buzz. He feels dazed and euphoric, filled with energy.

When he looks at Lily, she suddenly becomes the most beautiful mermaid in the world to him. She has big green fish eyes and pouty orange fish lips, long scaly ears that match her fins, glittery gills on her neck, flowing pink hair. Her breasts are bursting from a short yellow vinyl top, drawing his eyes. He's completely infatuated with her, forgetting all about Oona and the purpose of their visit. All he can think about is the strangely alluring woman sitting next to him.

The mermaid can tell that he's already under her spell, but the stimulation seems to be going both ways. Eliot realizes that his wings are shivering beneath his hoodie, releasing an intense amount of fairy dust. It's affecting the mermaid and causing her to be even more interested in him. She's not going to let him go without a fight.

Lily rubs his neck, pulling back his hood. Eliot tries to resist. He doesn't want to expose the antennae on his forehead. There aren't many races with antennae at his height, so it wouldn't be hard for her to deduce that he's a fairy just by revealing them. Even if she doesn't attack him for his race, he doesn't want to start a scene. He wonders if he shouldn't just get up and walk away.

"Oh, you have pink hair, too," she says, pulling back his hood just enough to reveal his pointed ear and the side of his spiky hair. "I love guys with pink hair. Can I see it?"

Before she can pull back his hood, Eliot holds it in place and shakes his head at her. "I'm sorry. I'd prefer to keep it on."

She frowns at him in a flirty way. "Aww... You're shy. That's so cute. I love shy boys. Are you a virgin?"

Eliot wonders if he should lie and tell her that he is. He might be able to get away with keeping his hood on if he pretends his behavior is due to being a shy young virgin who came to the brothel for his first time.

He finds himself saying, "Umm... Kind of ..."

It feels weird to lie about this. As a fairy, he's never had a problem having sex with almost anyone he wants to. He usually has to fight off the affection of everyone he meets. But if it helps the situation, he thinks it's worth a shot.

"That's so sweet," she says. "Do you want me to be your first time? I'll be gentle."

The second she says this, Eliot realizes he made a huge mistake. Now that she has the perfect opportunity to ask him to sleep with her, he's put himself in an awkward situation where he has to refuse. What's worse is that the intoxicating cocktail mixing with her mermaid pheromones is overwhelming his senses, he finds himself wanting to give in. His erection becomes so pronounced that it's impossible to hide. He's never slept with a mermaid before and would love to give it a try. Although he knows Oona would be mad at him and that it would put both of their lives in danger, he can't help but consider it.

"Umm.... I don't know..." It's the only response he can come up with to buy some time.

He has the money he was supposed to pay Oona for his tattoo work, which probably is enough to afford the prostitute, so it's possible that he could go through with it if he wanted to throw caution to the wind. He's never paid for sex in his life, but at the moment he doesn't have a problem giving in and trying it. He's always been interested in merfolk, not just octomaids. He's always been fascinated by the races who come from the sea. They are as strange and alien as they are beautiful. He sees them the same way that other people view fairies.

"You know you want to," the mermaid says, pressing her fishy orange lips against his cheek. "Let me show you paradise."

He shakes his head. "I can't..."

But despite his words, he finds himself moving closer to her. Letting her kiss his neck and suck on his ear. She pulls his hand to her fish tail, just below her belly button. As he rubs her, he realizes that he's touching her labia. It causes him to pull back, feeling awkward touching such a sexual area of her body. He knows that she won't let him get away without paying if she lets him touch her there. He has to stop this before it's too late.

But as he pulls his hand away, she forces it back in place. She holds his hand there until her labia becomes aroused. The scaly lips spread apart and release a cloud of fishy chemicals that covers his fingers. He can tell that his pheromones are increasing her sexual desire just as much as hers are affecting him.

"Come swim with me," Lily tells him. "I want you in my water."

As she pulls on him, Eliot thinks she's trying to pull him into the lagoon with the other mermaids. He notices a few other guys in the large indoor pool, swimming with the women in the water. The last thing he wants is to be exposed to the other people in the room. Even if he gave in to her charms and paid to sleep with her, he can't let anyone see him without his clothes on. He can't swim in the lagoon where everyone is watching.

"My cove isn't very far," she says. "Let me take you there."

She points at the waterways branching off from the lagoon. Mermaids are swimming hand-in-hand with their customers, taking them down indoor streams that lead to private coves. Because mermaids have a difficult time moving around outside the water, the only way to get to their rooms is to enter the lagoon and swim with them the whole way. There's no way that Eliot can go all the way with Lily unless he undresses in front of everyone.

Eliot looks at the piles of clothes at the edge of the lagoon. Along the wall to his left are rows of lockers where men are securing their belongings and changing into bathing suits. This is not something that Eliot can actually consider doing.

Lily rolls over onto Eliot's lap, her wet tail soaking through his pants. Her face is inches away from his, staring him in the eyes. The feeling of her body against him is strange. She's a lot heavier than he expected, pinning him into place on the bench. She undulates against him, grinding his erection through his pants.

She draws her scaly fingers across his lips and inserts two of them into his mouth. They taste of salt water but are also sweet like his intoxicating cocktail. He realizes that her hand is covered in her pheromones. She's trying to make sure he's full of them, preventing him from wanting to escape. She looks at him as if saying *you can't resist me, just give in.*

Oona told Eliot that mermaids are masters of seduction, but he didn't realize they were so aggressive. He didn't know just talking to one would end with her spread across his lap, shoving her vaginal fluids down his throat.

"Come on…" she says, smiling at him. "Swim with me."

Eliot spits out her fingers and says, "I want to, but seriously… I don't think—"

Before he finishes, she shoves her breasts into his face and says, "Stop being a pain. I won't settle for anyone else now that I have you in my grasp."

Eliot doesn't know what to say after that. He just sits there, awkwardly, waiting for somebody to come and save him.

"It'll be so amazing," she says. "I've always wanted to make love to a fairy."

When she says this, Eliot's eyes widen. He loses his erection. He wants to push her off of him and escape.

"I'm not a fairy..." he says.

She giggles at him. "Of course you are. I knew you were the second I saw you."

He tries to get out from under her, squirming to get away. Lily's tail slides off of him and plops onto the bench. She doesn't release her arms from around his shoulders though, she's not letting him get away so easily.

"You don't have to hide it from me," she says. "You might think all mermaids are racist toward fairies, but not me. I think fairies are hot. I always hoped one would come to see me one day."

Eliot can't believe it. He thought for sure she would kill him the second she found out his race, just as Oona had said. But he's happy he was wrong.

"You seriously don't care?" Eliot asks.

"Fuck no," she says.

Then she rips down his hood. As his antennae unfold, she sucks one of them into her mouth. He tenses up as it rubs against her tongue. His antennae are incredibly sensitive, three times that of his penis. He's never had anyone suck on his antennae before. It is both pleasurable and painful, causing him to whimper uncontrollably. He can't believe this is happening to him. He feels violated, but he can't help but enjoy the sensation. The suction of her fishy lips sends shivers throughout his body.

He jerks when she slurps his antennae one last time and then lets it go. She looks him in the eyes again and says, "Do you like that? Do you want me to continue?"

Eliot nods his head. He can't control himself. He's completely overwhelmed and lost in the moment. He could strip down to his underwear, release his wings, expose himself to everyone in the room, and he wouldn't care about the consequences.

"Three hundred dollars and I'll take you to heaven," she tells him.

Eliot is ready to go through with it, even digging his wallet out of his pants, when Oona calls out to him.

"Eliot, come on," Oona calls out from the other side of the lagoon.

When he sees the look of irritation on her face, Eliot loses his erection and comes to his senses. He pulls away from the mermaid, prying himself out of her grasp.

"I'm sorry, I have to go."

Lily's expression turns to anger, offended by his rejection.

As Eliot gets to his feet, she looks at Oona and back at Eliot.

"You like octomaids?" she asks.

As Eliot brushes the fishy slime from his pants, he nods his head and says, "I'm sorry."

But Lily doesn't take it very well. She glares at him with disgust and says, "Ewww…. That's so gross."

She pushes off the bench and slides backwards toward the water.

"I can't believe you'd choose a fucking spider over me."

Her eyes are so flustered that she looks like she's about to cry. As he goes to her, feeling apologetic and regretful, she just hisses at him and exposes a row of razor sharp teeth.

Eliot is paranoid she's going to call him out as a fairy, letting everyone know his secret, but she just keeps hissing at him until he backs off.

"Fuck off, insect," she yells at him as she enters the water. "Thanks for wasting my time."

Then she dives deep into the lagoon and disappears. Eliot wishes it wouldn't have gone this way. He really liked the pretty tropical mermaid and even thought maybe he'd come back to see her another time if everything turns out alright. But as Oona looks at him with fury in her eyes, he realizes that he shouldn't have even spoken to her in the first place. He steps away from the lagoon, shaking the pheromones from his body, feeling like a complete scumbag. He hopes Oona doesn't think less of him for his behavior.

CHAPTER
FIVE

Oona doesn't acknowledge his encounter with the mermaid. She just gives him a look of disappointment and shrugs it off, despite his soaking wet appearance and the look of overwhelming lust in his eyes. He wants to apologize to her as he approaches, but before he opens his mouth, she walks down a hallway away from the mermaid lagoon.

"Avia is this way," she tells him. "It took a while to get anyone to tell me where she was, but she still works here. Just stay back and stay out of trouble. I'll do all the talking."

They go to a room far away from the other customers and prostitutes. It's so out of the way that it seems like this friend of Oona's isn't one of the more popular women that work at Siren's Cove. He wonders if she isn't even a prostitute, but maybe somebody who works there for other reasons. Maybe she's an accountant or works security or something like that.

But as Oona knocks on the door to room 165 and Avia appears in the doorway, Eliot can tell that she definitely is another Siren's Cove prostitute. But she's not a mermaid.

"Hey Avia, can we come in?" Oona asks.

"Oona, is that you?" the woman says, completely shocked by their presence. "What the hell are you doing here?"

As they step through the door, Eliot gets a good look at Oona's friend. Avia is not exactly merfolk. She's a nixie, which is closer to Eliot's race than any of the Naiads in the building.

Nixies are related to fairykind, but they look nothing like other sprites. They are frog people, amphibians with smooth speckled skin and long gooey tongues.

"I haven't seen you in years," Avia says.

Eliot catches her eyes for a moment as he passes into the room, just before she closes the door behind them. Avia locks the door in a panic, as though terrified of anyone catching her in Oona's presence.

"They'd kill me if they saw me talking to you," the nixie says.

Avia is around Eliot's height, but with green and white striped skin, a short green bob haircut, loop earrings, a skimpy tank top and denim shorts. The room is half water and rustic wood flooring. A small pond the size of three hot tubs takes up a large section of the room, blanketed by lily pads and thick green pond scum. There is an entrance in the pool that most likely leads out to the lagoon in the main room, but it doesn't seem like it gets a lot of traffic. Nixies aren't known for being one of the more attractive races, not compared to fairies or mermaids. Avia probably has a very specific clientele that doesn't come to visit as regularly as the mermaid customers.

"We'll be gone soon," Oona tells her. "I don't want to be here any longer than we have to be."

Avia nods. Her breaths are heavy. She looks between Oona and Eliot, her thick green lips hanging open in distress.

"Why are you here?" Avia asks.

Oona slithers across the tile, looking around the room as if she's worried somebody might be hiding and listening. "We need your help."

Avia shakes her head. "It's not a good time. I haven't been able to meet my quota lately. They're talking about getting rid of me."

Oona nods, but doesn't seem too concerned with her friend's problems. She goes to the water and dips her tentacles in, wetting the octopus parts of her body.

"We need a place to lie low for a while," Oona says.

Avia goes to her, a confused look on her face. As Oona dips herself halfway into the sludgy frog water, her friend asks, "What did you do?"

Eliot thought there was no way that she'd fill her in on all the details, but Oona doesn't hesitate for a second.

"We killed Niko Kaji and are trying to blame it on the Naiads," Oona says as calmly as giving her the weather.

Her friend freaks out. "You did *what?*"

Eliot also can't believe she just spilled that info so casually. He doesn't know if this nixie woman is very trustworthy and it could be dangerous giving her all the details of their situation so easily. He doesn't know Avia, but she already seems far less trustworthy than it would have been to go to Tiki and Taka.

"Him and his friends are in pieces out back," Oona says. "We need to get out of here before anyone finds them."

Avia's mouth drops open. She looks around as though terrified of her own surroundings. "That's crazy. Do you have a death wish or what?"

Oona shrugs. "It was unavoidable. They were starting shit in Nuri's club and had to be dealt with."

Her words only make Avia more nervous. "Does Madam Nuri know about this? She doesn't seem like somebody who would cause trouble for the Naiads."

Oona shakes her head. "No, she doesn't know. She can't know. We need to blame the Naiads for this. Otherwise we're dead."

Avia backs away, a terrified look in her eyes. "You can't do that. Everything is tense right now. The Naiads are killing anyone for the slightest infraction these days. If they find out I'm involved…"

Oona dunks herself in the water. When she comes up, she's covered in algae. "Why do you care? The Avia I know would love to watch the Naiads squirm."

Avia shakes her head. "That was ages ago. I'm just trying to survive now. It's not the way it was when you were here."

"Relax," Oona tells her. "We don't need to get you involved. We just need you to get us out of here. You said if I ever needed your help you'd give me a place to hide out. Is that still an option? Or did you forget about all the times that I saved your ass?"

Avia turns away. She takes a few deep breaths. "I didn't forget. I'll help you. But I can't leave."

The nixie goes to the bed on the far side of the room. She opens a drawer in the nightstand and pulls out a set of keys.

"You can borrow my car, but don't let anyone see you using it," Avia says.

"Can we use your apartment for the night?" Oona asks. "I don't want to go home until this all blows over."

Avia looks down. "I don't have an apartment anymore. I live here. It's not like the old times. They don't let any of the workers stay off premises. I can only leave a few hours a week."

Oona steps out of the water, dripping sludgy liquid onto the wood floor. "Fucking Marius…"

"He's gotten even worse in the past year," Avia says. "You're lucky you left when you did."

Oona's eyes narrow. "You should have left with me. Madam Nuri is a lot more reasonable than Marius."

Avia looks away. "Yeah, but she wouldn't have me. You've got abilities that interested her. I'm just a whore. Madam Nuri has no use for a frog whore."

Oona goes to her and holds her hand against the nixie's cheek. "You're more than a whore. You're the only person that kept me sane when I was here."

As they stare longingly in each other's eyes, Eliot begins to feel uncomfortable standing there. It appears as though the two were once lovers a long time ago. Eliot wonders if the reason Oona has never shown sexual attraction to him, despite the fact that he's a fairy who is irresistible to women, is because she isn't attracted to men at all. He wonders if she was in love with Avia all this time. But as soon as Oona places her hand on Avia's shoulder, Avia pushes it away, treating her like an older sister who doesn't understand what it's like to live in her shadow.

"Whatever…" Avia says. "Just take my car and don't get me involved in your bullshit."

Oona nods and steps back. "Thank you, Avia. It means a lot that you still care."

"Just get out of here before anyone thinks I'm involved. I have enough problems."

Oona just takes the keys and slithers away from her friend. "I'll bring your car back in a few days, once it's safe."

Avia just laughs at her words. "If you live that long."

Oona goes to Eliot and pushes him toward the door.

Before they leave, Oona looks back at her old friend and says, "I'm sorry I left you here. I just couldn't stay for anything. Not after what Marius did."

Avia shrugs. "I'm happy for you."

But the words come out with venom, as though the nixie had only bitterness left for her old friend. She just goes back to her pond and hops onto a lily pad, refusing to say goodbye to her visitors. Her croaks are more like weeps as she curls up and ignores them leaving her room.

As they move quickly toward the exit of the brothel, Eliot feels a new sense of anxiety. But it's not his anxiety, it's coming from Oona. She's not the same confident, put-together octomaid she was only moments ago.

"This isn't good," she tells him as she pushes him toward the exit.

"What isn't good?" he asks.

Oona doesn't answer until they get out of the club and into the parking lot, away from curious ears.

She says, "Avia was different from the last time I saw her. I thought she'd be happy to escalate the war between the Sylphs and Naiads, but she's scared. Scared people do desperate things."

Eliot is surprised she would have trusted her friend with their situation if she knew of her friend's condition. "Why did you tell her about Niko if we were only going to borrow her car? She didn't need to know."

"I thought she would have helped more if she knew. The old Avia would have done everything she could to make sure Niko's death was blamed on the Naiads. She used to want nothing more than to destroy the Naiad family."

"But not anymore?"

"I'm worried she'll go straight to Marius and tell him everything she knows. Or worse, she might go to Madam Nuri and tell her everything in order to free herself from Naiad control."

Eliot thinks about it. He's paranoid that coming here was the worst thing they could have done. Even if they walked all the way home it would've been better than spilling all their secrets to a woman who might betray them. They could have even convinced Tiki and Taka to help and it would've been better.

"So what do we do now?" Eliot asks.

They get to a small green car in the parking lot and open the doors. Eliot jumps right into the passenger seat without making sure nobody was watching. Oona looks around for a moment before slipping inside.

"We can't go home," she says. "If Avia tells anyone we're involved, my apartment will be the first place to be searched."

"What about my place?" Eliot asks, almost excited by the idea of having Oona over.

She shakes her head. "We should stay in a hotel. I have a credit card under a fake name for just such an emergency. Nobody will know where to find us."

Eliot nods his head. He is even more interested in staying

at a hotel with Oona than at one of their apartments. Even though his life is in danger, he can't help but get excited about their current situation.

Oona rents a hotel room with her phone, one that they can access without ever showing their faces to anyone. She drives them across town, outside both Naiad and Sylph territory. When they get to the room, they type in a code on the door handle and are let right in.

"You don't have to work tomorrow do you?" Oona asks.

Eliot shakes his head. "Tomorrow's my day off."

Eliot can't stop shaking as he steps inside the room with the woman of his dreams. He can tell he's still overwhelmed with mermaid pheromones. Everything that enters his mind is sexual. He fantasizes about Oona, wishing that she was as aggressive toward him as the mermaid back at the brothel. But when he looks at her, he can tell that sex is the farthest thing from her mind. She only cares about survival at this moment. They are only here to hide out from those who might want to kill them.

Oona enters the bathroom and turns on the faucet, filling the tub with water. As she does this, Eliot looks around the room. It's not very large. There's only one queen-sized bed and a table with two chairs. There's a television but it's a decade old and probably doesn't play anything but the local channels.

"The place isn't bad," Eliot says. "I thought it would be a shithole."

When the bath is full, Oona slides into it, wetting her tentacles. She doesn't seem very pleased with her bath. It isn't full of salt water as she would prefer. Merfolk need to wet themselves on a regular basis, regardless of whether they soak in salt water or fresh water, but none of the species are happy when they have to resort to using a bathtub to wet themselves. They prefer natural rivers or lakes or oceans or even properly maintained aquariums, but never a bathtub.

Eliot is so drugged up that he can't help but stand in the doorway and watch Oona with lust-filled eyes. She doesn't take her clothes off while bathing, she just sits there, her tentacles squirming against the porcelain.

"I brought my tattoo equipment," Oona tells him. "I'd like to finish the piece we started today."

Eliot nods. He didn't even consider the possibility of getting tattooed again. The thought of it fills him with anticipation.

Oona continues, "We'll be here for a while, so any work you need done will be a good way to pass the time."

Eliot smiles. He's happy about this turn of events. But as the good news hits him, he also starts to worry about their future. He isn't sure what they plan to do besides stay in the hotel for the night.

"How long do we need to stay here?" Eliot asks. "Will we be able to go home in the morning?"

Oona seems almost annoyed by the question. She dunks her head in the water and then lets the fluid drain down her chest.

"If it's okay with you, I'd like to stay for a few days," Oona says. "I was supposed to take a vacation for the next couple of days, so I won't be expected back at the Snake Pit. It would be better to wait and see what happens. As long as Avia doesn't give us up, we should be fine."

Eliot nods, but then thinks about it. "What happens if she does give us up?"

Oona takes a deep breath and then pulls the plug to start draining the bathtub.

"We'll have to get out of the city," she says. "Run as far away as we can and hope they lose interest in us."

Eliot leans against the wall of the bathroom, too dizzy to stay upright. "Is it possible that they'll lose interest in us if they know we killed Niko?"

Oona stands up, water draining from her tentacles onto the bathroom floor.

"Shino Kaji will blame the Naiads no matter what they find out about us," she says. "It's really Madam Nuri we have to worry about. The good thing about her is that she will go for the easiest possible solution to her problems. If we are out of her reach, we won't be available to use as a sacrifice. She'll have to figure something else out."

Eliot nods, but isn't quite sure that everything will work out as she says. He has to trust that she knows what she's talking about.

"The worst case scenario, we'll have to leave town and never come back," she says.

Eliot feels a bit relieved by her words, even though he's terrified by the idea of leaving town and never coming back. But at the same time, he likes the idea of being on the run with Oona. There's a part of him that wishes it would never end. He'd be happier than ever to spend the rest of his life with her, even if it was only as an accomplice.

Oona doesn't dry herself off after leaving the bathroom, dripping water all over the hotel room carpet. Eliot backs away to give her room, but can't keep his eyes off of her. She's magnificent to watch with her glistening tentacles and wet braless t-shirt. And with the aphrodisiac still in his system, it doesn't take much to excite him.

Eliot takes off his hoodie and places it by his backpack, letting his wings loose to spread out and flap in the cool air. It feels good to let his fairy side out again. He flutters his wings, drying the moisture that had built up on them from his time at Siren's Cove.

"Lie down on the bed," Oona tells him. "It shouldn't take long to finish the piece I was working on."

Eliot looks at her with a bright smile on his face. "Seriously? Right now?"

She nods and points at the left side of the bed. "Take off all your clothes. You can use a towel from the bathroom if you need to cover up a little."

Eliot is so drugged up and full of lust that he doesn't hesitate to comply. He doesn't even bother with getting a towel and just strips naked in front of her, lying down on the bed, waiting to be tattooed.

She takes a while to get her equipment in order. During this time, Eliot begins to feel awkward. He decides that it would be best to go get a towel. He doesn't want Oona to get the wrong idea. But before he's able to get up, Oona comes to him with the needle, ready to get to work. Eliot might have missed his opportunity to cover himself. She puts all of her equipment on the nightstand next to him.

"Are you ready?" she asks.

Eliot nods, but he's far from ready. His body is completely exposed, his penis hanging out right in front of her. He's so turned on at the moment that it wouldn't take much for him to get an erection. And if that happens right in front of Oona, without even a small piece of fabric to cover it up, he will be beyond embarrassed.

Oona rubs his lower abdomen with alcohol. An almost aggravated expression is on her face as she scrubs, sensing the mermaid pheromones that cover this area of his body. Eliot forgot about how angry Oona gets when he doesn't keep his tattoos clean. The mermaid water that coats his body is full of bacteria that likely infected his open tattoo wounds. He really shouldn't have let Lily spread herself across his body if he cared about keeping his new tattoo clean. It was probably the worst thing he could have done to it, since mermaids are known to be covered in highly infectious microbes and parasites. Luckily,

Oona doesn't criticize him for it and just rubs the area clean.

The second she finishes cleaning, she turns the needle on and gets to work. Eliot can't handle his penis lying there exposed, inches away from her needle, so he covers it with his hands and tries to relax.

As she tattoos him, Oona says, "If we end up staying here for a few days I hope to finish you. It'll pass the time for us. Even if you don't have the money yet, I'd like to do it all. You can pay me back whenever you can. That is, if we survive all of this."

Eliot smiles when she says this. The idea of being tattooed by her for three straight days makes him happier than he's been in months. But after a few minutes, his happiness turns to depression. He doesn't like the idea of Oona being finished with him. He wants to be tattooed by her forever. He's always seen himself as her canvas, but the idea that one day there will be no canvas left to be tattooed is a distressing thought to Eliot. He never wants it to end.

As Oona works on his lower abdomen, Eliot's brain floods with endorphins. Already influenced by aphrodisiacs and pheromones, Eliot's arousal is even stronger than previous times that he was tattooed. His penis becomes erect in his hands and his wings quiver behind his back.

"I shouldn't be too long," Oona says, aware of his situation.

But the sensation is so pleasurable that Eliot can't help but moan out loud. He wants nothing more than for her to pull his hands away and drive her needle right into the shaft of his penis, tattooing his member until it explodes. But as Eliot's thighs squeeze together with anticipation, Oona moves on, tattooing away from his penis, closer to his belly button.

The antennae on his forehead stick straight up as she cuts into his flesh. He can't help but quiver and pulsate against her touch, his arousal increasing with every inch of needlework embedded in his skin.

Oona's tentacles slither against his flesh as she gets closer to completion. The suction cups don't latch onto his skin as they usually do. Instead, her tentacles slide up and down his chest, stimulated by the nearly completed design. Oona looks the happiest she's been all day, and Eliot wants the octomaid to enjoy the moment. His penis stabs into the palm of his hand, exited by Oona's passion and determination to finish her work.

"Hold still…" she says to prevent Eliot from squirming any further.

She licks her lips and tattoos him all the way to completion. When she finishes, Oona leans back with satisfaction, admiring her finished piece on Eliot's body.

Eliot looks down at the eel design, loving every inch of it. He can tell that a lot of Oona's emotions went into it. The art is much better than he imagined, maybe even the best design she ever put on his body.

"I want to keep going if that's okay with you," she tells him.

"Isn't it finished?" Eliot asks.

Oona's deep black eyes lock onto his. "I want to do another one before the night's over. Can I tattoo lower?"

Eliot nods before he realizes that she's pointing at his crotch. He was uncomfortable with the idea of the eel design on his lower abdomen opening its mouth as if swallowing his penis, so he kind of wants to see how it ends up. Maybe she'll do something not so crude and lowbrow.

She removes his hands from his penis, exposing it to the cold hotel room air, and gets to work. But she doesn't tattoo his genitals as he thought she was going to. Instead she addresses the area along the side of his pubic region.

"This area is sensitive," she tells him. "Just bear with me for an hour or so."

Eliot nods, but when she starts tattooing he tenses up, curling his fingers into fists, feeling more vulnerable under her needle than he's ever felt before. His penis stays erect despite how much he tries to calm himself. He tries to move it away so that it stops poking into Oona's hand as she works. He closes his eyes, pretending it's not happening. He's never felt more embarrassed.

"I'm sorry about that..." Eliot tells her, worried that she'll be offended by his erection getting in her way.

But she doesn't even acknowledge his words. One of her tentacles slides against his stomach and curls around his penis. Oona is just trying to move it out of the way like a gas station attendant might move a window wiper while cleaning a car windshield, but the sensation is so intense that it drives Eliot into orgasmic pleasure. He writhes against her hold, squirming in the bed.

When Oona realizes what she's doing, she releases her tentacle from him and continues her work, her mind completely absorbed in the new piece of art. Eliot bites his finger as hard as he can to ease his erection, preventing him from exploding all over the place.

When the new piece is complete, Oona releases herself from the fairy's body.

Eliot takes a few deep breaths, looks down at his crotch, and says, "I love it." Even though she just tattooed some abstract scale-like designs around his penis that don't appear to be a part of a finished image. Oona probably has plans to incorporate them into other works in that part of his body. It is just a filler tattoo until she works on his penis and upper thighs.

"I'm done for tonight," she says. "But I'll continue in the morning."

Eliot nods. Whatever works for her is okay with him.

"What do we do now?" Eliot asks, looking up at the enormous octomaid hovering over him.

Oona leans back. "There's only one bed. You can have it. I'd prefer to sleep in the bathtub anyway."

When Eliot hears her say this, he thinks she sounds annoyed by having to sleep in the tub. Even though she normally sleeps in water, he can't help but imagine she'd prefer the comfort of a bed.

"Are you sure?" he asks. "You can take the bed if you want." After he says this, he realizes he has an alternative motive to his question. He can't help himself and adds, "It's a large bed. I'd be happy to share it with you if you don't want to sleep in the bathtub."

Eliot would love to share a bed with Oona. Even if nothing happened, the idea of sleeping so close to her would be a dream come true. He knows that merfolk don't actually sleep in beds, but he still likes the idea of it becoming a reality. He thinks it's worth asking even if she turns him down.

Oona stares at him, scanning his body up and down. She doesn't say anything for a moment, leaving them in an uncomfortable silence.

Then she asks, "Are you trying to have sex with me?"

Eliot's eyes pop open and he backs away from her. He's surprised she would bring that up. Despite the fact that he wants to have sex with her more than anything, he wasn't suggesting that. He just wanted to offer it to her as he would anyone he was trying to be nice to.

"No, not at all…" he finds himself saying. "I just thought the bed was big enough for both of us."

Oona brushes off his words and says, "I don't normally fuck my customers. It goes against my standards."

Eliot shakes his head, terrified that he's acting like a creep. He says, "I understand. I'm sorry I brought it up."

But as he says this, his heart sinks into his chest. He so wishes that Oona felt differently about him. He wishes she didn't just see him as a customer, but as somebody she might be able to fall in love with. She is the most perfect girl he's ever met and he wants more than anything for her to see him as more than just flesh that she can deposit her art upon.

Oona slithers away from the bed. She says, "The bathtub will be better for me. I'm tired. I'm going to need to go to sleep for a while."

Eliot nods. He completely understands that an octomaid would prefer a tub versus a bed. She needs to keep her tentacles wet. It must be impossible to be comfortable in sheets where they could dry out and become flaky.

"I'll come back later," she says, slithering across the carpet to the bathroom.

Once she leaves the room, Eliot lies down, his wings flapping behind his back. He feels embarrassed. Even though he didn't actually ask Oona to have sex with him, she knew right away what he was hoping for. He feels like such an idiot. Of course it's not the time to push their relationship into sexual territory. Maybe once Oona finishes tattooing her art across every inch of his body, but not during the crisis that he caused for both of them. At the moment, he should just be happy that she wants to have anything to do with him. He created the whole mess that she's in. He should be happy that she still wants to be by his side through this whole ordeal.

Eliot lies in the dark, trying to sleep. He turns onto his stomach so that his wings can spread out and wave in the cool hotel air conditioning. He's still aroused by the encounter with the mermaid as well as the two tattoo sessions with Oona. Although the situation he's in is dire and he should be terrified for his life, he can't help but feel excited about it. He's never spent so much time with Oona before. He knows that no matter what, he's sure to have a closer relationship with her when this is all over.

He should feel that his predicament is dangerous, maybe even hopeless, but with Oona involved he can't help but believe it will all be okay. She's the most competent person he's ever met. If anyone can get through this kind of situation unscathed it's her. He's sure everything will turn out fine.

As he falls asleep, Eliot dreams of erotic things. He lies naked in a pool of thick black liquid, his body writhing in the goo. His wings become wet and sticky, fluttering in the fluid. He's not sure where it all came from, but for some reason he knows exactly what it is. The liquid is Oona's ink, freshly squeezed from her and still warm. Eliot bathes in it, her salty fish aroma covering his skin, feeling as though he's swimming inside of her.

Tentacles emerge from the black fluid and curl around his legs and arms, wrapping him up tightly until he can't move anymore. There's no sign of the rest of Oona, just her tentacles. They move up his chest and coil around his throat. His body transforms into a woman's and the tentacles twist around his breasts, sliding down between his legs. He spreads his thighs, allowing the tentacles to slither against his shaven pubic region. His pelvis pushes upward, begging to be penetrated by the oily appendages, but they just keep moving, exploring his body. He squirms against their touch as the suction cups adhere to his labia and begin to suck. Eliot squeals and wriggles at the sensation. He tells her to fuck him, but she doesn't hear. Oona isn't really there. It's just the octopus part of her body, each tentacle moving independently as though each one has a mind of its own.

Eliot wakes up in a pool of sweat, his penis so erect that it hurts. He touches his chest, feeling for phantom breasts that aren't there anymore. It was just a dream. He's still in his masculine form. When he looks around the dark room, he realizes that the place has been flooded with his pheromones. It must have happened in his sleep. The air is so thick with them that he has a difficult time breathing. He's never released this much fairy dust before.

Without thinking what he's doing, he finds himself putting his hand down his pants and grabbing his penis tightly. He strokes it a few times, ready to jerk himself off right there. His eyes close tight as he caresses himself, moaning louder than he should with Oona in the bathroom next to him.

His eyes pop open the second he hears her. Oona stands at the edge of the bed, looking down at him.

"Oh, I'm sorry…" Eliot tells her, pulling himself upright. "I didn't see you there."

Oona doesn't say anything. She was there the whole time, watching him. She slides closer and Eliot realizes that she's not wearing her top, she's completely naked in the shadows of the room.

"Are you okay?" Eliot asks.

She seems to be in a trance. She stares down at him, wide-eyed, rubbing her breast with one tentacle. As she gets closer, Eliot realizes what's wrong. She's been drugged by the thick pheromones in the room, overwhelmed with lust. There's a hunger in her eyes that Eliot's never seen before. She doesn't look at him like another living being, but as a piece of meat that she wants to feed upon.

"I'm sorry about releasing so much fairy dust," Eliot says. "I couldn't control it in my sleep. I'll open a window."

But before he can get out of the bed, Oona wraps a tentacle around his waist and pulls him closer. He finds himself unable to move, her tentacle squeezing tightly around his abdomen, the suction cups leaving dark red circles on his chest.

"Oona?" he asks.

Eliot wonders if she's even aware of what she's doing. She clearly said that she would never sleep with one of her clients, that it went against her standards. Eliot is sure that she's not in control of her actions. But he's not in any better of a position. He doesn't put up a fight as Oona wraps him up in her limbs and strips him naked.

"Do you know what you're doing?" Eliot asks her. "Do you know where you are?"

But she still doesn't answer. She just pulls off his clothes and flings them away, lifting him up in the air. Eliot's wanted nothing more than to experience this moment, to make love to the woman he's been infatuated with for so long. But it doesn't feel right. He feels like he's taking advantage of her, even though she's the one who's trying to have sex with him. Even still, he can't get himself to stop this from happening, despite knowing it's not really what she wants. The ecstasy flooding his mind forces him to just go with it, enjoying every second of it.

Oona crawls on top of Eliot, her tentacles pulling up the sheets, pressing her pelvis to his. She's warm and oily and smooth against his naked flesh. Feeling the area between her tentacles sends shivers through his body. He can't believe this is really happening. He squirms and grips the bedding in his little fingers.

She's enormous compared to him. Her weight is not nearly as heavy as he would expect at her size, but he feels buried beneath her. Oona's tentacles curl around his body, hugging him and covering his skin with her fishy mucus. He looks up at her searching for connection in her eyes. But she isn't really acknowledging him. She is focused more on the art tattooed in his skin. She's having sex with her own artwork. Her tentacles slide across her designs, following the patterns from his stomach up to his neck. She leans in and kisses his nipple, licking the fish scale tattoo on his left pectoral muscle, tracing it in a circle all the way to his armpit.

As Eliot opens his mouth to speak, she shoves a tentacle down his throat, forcing him to keep quiet as she admires her art. He gags as she thrusts the tentacle deeper, tickling the back of his tongue and his uvula. He finds himself sucking on it, giving the oily appendage a blowjob despite it seeming to do nothing to pleasure her. He reaches up to grab her breast. It's massive compared to his hand and he's only able to grasp a third of it in one squeeze. A tentacle wraps around his wrist and pulls it away. Another tentacle coils up his other wrist.

Oona restrains both of his arms against the mattress as she lowers herself down his body, rubbing against his erection. When he feels her vulva touching the head of his penis, he is surprised by the sensation. Her genitals are far more octopus than human, rubbery and slimy and covered in bumps and grooves. Like a lower mouth, her vagina opens up and swallows his penis, sucking him into a cavity of thick mucus. His penis feels completely lost inside her slimy tunnel. But it's strangely pleasurable. It feels like she is sucking his whole body into her as she pulsates on top of him.

She kisses his neck and shoulders, licking his skin as if to taste the flavor of her ink contained within it. She rubs her tentacles all over his body, the hundreds of tiny suction cups on the innermost areas of her appendages throbbing like miniature mouths.

His wings won't stop flittering as she fucks him. His entire body vibrates. This is everything he's ever desired. He gives himself to her completely and, as she shoves her tentacle deeper down his throat, he feels nothing but pleasure. His body tensing and tingling. The pressure building until, at last, he explodes in ecstasy. Every muscle in his body spasming and releasing. At the same moment, Oona arches her back and sprays him with ink. As she climaxes, she tightens her oily appendages around his body, applying so much pressure that all the air is forced out of his lungs and he can no longer breathe. Then she lets out a moan and collapses on top of him.

Eliot lies there, her body encompassing him. Her tentacles slithering up and down his tattooed flesh as she falls deep into sleep. He feels trapped beneath her, unable to move despite how much he needs to use the bathroom. Nevertheless, he can't help but smile at the sensation. Her weight on top of him, her breasts against his bare chest, as she breathes heavily and drools down his shoulder. It's perhaps the happiest he's been in years, maybe ever. He wraps his arms around her and closes his eyes, wishing the moment would last forever.

CHAPTER
SIX

They wake up next to each other in the morning. Oona is beside him, her tentacles still wrapped around his arms and waist. His body is coated in her slime and ink. His left wing's stuck to her right breast, glued in place by her sweat and mucus. When their eyes meet, Oona just glares at him, a confused expression on her face. She puts her hand between her tentacles, feeling her vagina for signs of male ejaculate.

"What the hell happened?" she asks in a calm yet firm tone, sniffing her sticky fingers. "Did we have sex?"

Eliot feels so guilty that he doesn't know what to say. He wonders if he should act as surprised as she is. He didn't have much choice when she attacked him during the night, but he knows that it was all his fault.

He feigns ignorance and asks, "You don't remember?"

She shakes her head, pulling her tentacles away from his body and peeling his wing from her chest. She gets out of the bed and goes toward the bathroom.

"I think I released too many pheromones in my sleep," he explains. "You crawled into the bed with me. I thought you wanted to…"

But Oona doesn't say anything. She disappears into the bathroom and turns the shower on, trying to wash the fairy spunk out of her crotch.

"I'm sorry…" Eliot calls out, but he's not sure she can hear him.

He lies in bed, pulling the covers up, feeling like a complete scumbag. Although he had no control over his pheromones, especially while he slept, he wonders if Oona will blame him for it. She might think he drugged her, which wouldn't be far from the truth. Fairy pheromones are a powerful aphrodisiac that are considered irresistible to most races. He's never taken advantage of anyone, but he could any time he wanted to if he was that kind of guy. He could have used his pheromones on Oona ever since the day he fell in love with her, but that's not something he ever wanted to do. He wanted her to be with him of her own free will. But after this, he's sure she'll never like him in that way. She'll always see him as the scumbag who drugged her and took advantage of the situation, despite the fact that she was the one who practically molested him in his sleep.

Eliot looks around for his clothes, thinking it would be appropriate to at least put his pants on. But before he can dig them out of the blankets, Oona returns from the bathroom, dripping water all over the carpeting. She crawls back into the bed with him, pulls the cover up and lies back, resting her head against the headboard.

Not sure what else to do, Eliot relaxes and lies back down. They sit in silence for a while. It feels good to be next to her, despite the situation. Her body radiates against his skin, making him feel calm and comfortable. He lets go of the awkwardness and tries to enjoy the moment. Lying in bed next to her is almost more enjoyable than the sex they had last night. One of her tentacles curls around his leg, squeezing it firmly as though giving him a loving embrace.

"I remember a little now," she says, breaking the silence. "It wasn't your fault. I'm ovulating. Octomaids can't control themselves while they're ovulating, especially at my age."

Eliot still feels guilty. He shakes his head and says, "But if it wasn't for my stupid pheromones…" He pauses, not sure what else to say but, "I'm sorry."

"Don't be sorry," she says, two more tentacles slithering up his chest, as though petting him. "It was nice. I'm glad we did it." She turns to him and looks him in the eyes. "I've never slept with anyone like you before."

He's not sure if he should be happy or concerned by her words. Does she mean because he's a fairy or because he's different from other guys? Because he's younger and smaller? Either way, he's wondering if it should be something that he should be insulted by.

"I'm just worried that we didn't use protection," she says.

"Because of my sentient blood?

Oona shakes her head, "I'm more worried about being pregnant. I'm not ready to produce offspring. There's still things I want to do with my life."

Eliot's eyes narrow at her words. He wasn't even thinking about that possibility. Although Oona is the one person he might consider having children with, he didn't want to burden her with this. They aren't even dating.

"Can fairies and octomaids even reproduce?" he asks. He's never heard of a fairy octomaid hybrid so assumed it was not a possibility.

She nods her head. "It's not common for us to mate outside our race, but we can breed with most races. Fairies, elves, humans… it's been known to happen."

"I've never heard of it before…"

"The women of our species do sometimes, but our offspring are always octomaid. There aren't any half-breeds. It is hypothesized that men of our species can produce half-octomaid offspring with other races, but I've never heard of it happening before. Males of my kind are sexually repulsed by other species, so they never mate outside of our race."

Eliot nods his head. He's never heard of this before. Octomaids are not a very common race in the civilized world, so he's never met any besides Oona. He's never even seen an adult male, even in photographs.

"What will you do if you are pregnant?" Eliot asks.

Although it must be a scary and horrible thought for her, Eliot can't help but feel a little excited by the idea. Even if she never falls in love with him, there's a deep urge inside of him that stirs at the idea of impregnating her. He's delighted by the thought of having octomaid children. He'd love to be connected to her forever by blood.

"Octomaids aren't capable of terminating their pregnancies," she says. "I'd have to go through the process of having them despite my personal desires."

Eliot nods his head. He doesn't know what to say. The idea that he might have impregnated Oona is beginning to turn him on. His penis becomes erect. He wants to just roll over and make love with her again, just to make sure she's pregnant with his offspring.

"It will be terrible," Oona says. "I'm not ready to die."

When Eliot hears this, he becomes confused. His erection begins to fade. "What do you mean? Why would you worry about dying?"

"Octomaids only live for a few months after giving birth," she says. "Our bodies expend everything to grow the young. It's why our race doesn't live very long. Once we know we're pregnant, we return to the sea, give birth to our brood, and then die soon afterward. It's the lifecycle of an octomaid. We are different from other species in this way. Other merfolk, like mermaids and sharkmaids, get to live to see their young grow up. But not us. It's a curse, and one of the main reasons we prefer a solitary life. It's why I've always avoided serious relationships."

When Eliot hears this, his heart sinks. His excitement vanishes and is replaced with guilt. If he's impregnated her, it means that she'll die. It means that he'll be responsible for killing the woman he loves. It would be the worst thing that could ever happen.

"Oh my god…" Eliot cries, he sits up, wanting to console her. "I'm so sorry. I had no idea. Had I known, maybe…"

Oona just brushes his words away. "Don't worry about it. We don't know that I'm pregnant. We only had sex once."

Eliot shakes his head. "You don't understand. I'm a fairy. We have very powerful reproductive systems compared to other races. Fairy women ovulate for 20 days a month. And the sperm of fairy men is incredibly potent and can survive for weeks. Any time we have sex without condoms it almost always results in pregnancy. We can't just *hope* that you didn't get pregnant. It's almost a certainty. We have to do something about it."

"What can we do?" Oona asks.

Eliot straightens his posture, looking around the room. "We at least have to get spermicidal jelly. If we're really lucky and you're not pregnant already, that's the only way to kill any of the sperm that might still be in there. Otherwise conception could occur tomorrow or even weeks from now."

Oona can't help but laugh. "Sounds like a pain in the ass. I feel sorry for girls of your kind."

Her laughter catches Eliot off guard. He's never heard her laugh before. He didn't even know that octomaids were capable of having a sense of humor.

"I didn't know that fairies pop out babies left and right," she says. "I heard that they rarely have more than one or two children."

When she says this, Eliot can't believe she's so nonplussed by what he told her. She seems to be taking the news better than Eliot, more interested in fairy biology than the implications it has on her own body. It's as though she's already accepted the consequences, even if the worst case scenario might be true.

"We don't usually have more than one child," Eliot says. "It's very easy for us to conceive, but it's incredibly difficult for the pregnancies to come to term."

"Why's that?" she asks.

"Fairy fetuses are known to self-terminate," he explains. "During pregnancy, neither parent may experience any stress or anxiety, nor depression or anger. Unless fairy parents are full of love and happiness at all times, the fetus will refuse to come into the world. It's the natural order of our kind. It prevents us from having children when we don't want them or when we aren't in a good place in our lives to have them. Fairies want to live in a world filled with love, so much so that without it, we'd rather not be born. Everything has to be emotionally perfect. It's why most fairies, even married couples trying to have a baby, will go through many miscarriages before a single child is born. It's difficult to have a second child, and nearly impossible to have a third, due to the stress caused by raising even one."

"So it's the complete opposite of octomaids," Oona says. "We have trouble conceiving, but once we do, there's no way to stop it. You have children easily, but have a hard time giving birth. It sounds like both of our species are cursed."

Eliot nods. He finds it difficult to accept that their species are even compatible with each other. He wishes it was impossible for them to interbreed. If that were true then it wouldn't put Oona in danger of dying from their night of passion.

"Maybe it's a good thing," he says.

She looks at him, her big black eyes digging into his. "What is?"

"Maybe because of my fairy DNA your pregnancy will be terminated and you won't have to die. You know, if it ends up that you actually are pregnant."

Oona shakes her head. "It doesn't work that way. Even if the pregnancy is terminated, it will still mean that I will die. The second after conception an octomaid's body begins to deteriorate. It'll just mean that I'll die for nothing."

Eliot lowers his eyes, even more disturbed by the situation. He wishes there was more that he could do. It's all his fault. If only he knew more about octomaid biology before they had sex.

"We shouldn't worry about it, though," Oona says. "It's unlikely we're going to survive for much longer anyway."

Eliot looks at her, surprised that she'd speak with so little hope.

"I never should have trusted Avia," she says. "I had no idea she would have changed so much." She lies back, rubbing water from her eyes. "I never thought I'd see her so afraid."

Although she just wants to go back to sleep, Eliot urges her to get some spermicidal jelly. He tells her that he'll go get it for her, but she insists on going herself. She says that she has to ditch Avia's car anyway and doesn't trust Eliot with the task.

"Get a pregnancy test, too," Eliot says.

"Why?" Oona asks. "They don't work unless I use it after I miss my period."

Eliot shakes his head. "Try getting a pregnancy test for fairies. They work immediately."

"Even if I'm not a fairy?"

"It's worth trying," he says. "If it is negative it might not necessarily mean you're in the clear. But if it comes up positive..."

"Fine..." she says.

Eliot only wants her to take it so that he can feel a little better about himself, make him relax a little if it's negative, make him feel hopeful that he didn't actually cause the end of her life.

Oona gets dressed and leaves the motel room. She tells him not to go anywhere or look out the window, not even for a second, and he agrees. But the moment she leaves the room, he goes straight to the window and watches her slither down the stairs toward the vehicle. He prays that it's not the last time he ever sees her. He watches until she gets into the car and drives away. If she notices him watching her, she doesn't look back.

When Eliot turns around, he sees the bed is coated in slime and black ink. The room reeks of a dead fish, an odor that surely has permeated the mattress and all the soft furnishings. He feels embarrassed of the mess they'll leave behind when they check out. There isn't anything he can do to make it any better. The housekeeping staff are surely going to be irritated to have to clean it up.

Despite how disgusting it looks, Eliot can't help but crawl back into bed and embrace the fishy puddle of goo. It's still warm from Oona's body, still smells of her. He flutters his wings as he inhales the scent, remembering the passionate night he had with her. But he still can't help but hate himself for how it turned out. If he could take it all back, he would. He would even have given Niko a blowjob if it would've prevented all this. He would take back every tattoo on his body, every moment he ever spent with Oona, if it would save her life. But all he can do now is hope everything will be fine. All he can do is pray that they both survive.

As he sits alone in the room, Eliot wonders what childhood for Oona must have been like. Before his parents died, Eliot had a wonderful childhood. He had a loving mother and father who would do anything for him, who surrounded him with so much affection that it was nearly suffocating. But Oona must have never known her parents. Her mother must have just dropped her off on the ocean floor and then died soon afterward, forcing her to survive on her own in a hostile environment.

Eliot wonders if octomaids are close to their siblings. He wonders if they form a bond with each other when they are young or just go their separate ways. They might even be cannibalistic and eat each other to survive. If this is true it would make sense that others see them as cold and heartless. Most people never trust the races that are born in the deep dark sea, but Eliot feels empathy for them. He can only imagine how hard it would be to grow up in such a loveless environment. They must all have such horrible childhoods.

He knows that many of them find their ways to the surface and join the civilized world, either by being adopted into a loving home or by joining a street gang of similar merfolk children. But for every one that enters society, there are ten more that never leave the oceans. Most of them are killed by predators or by swimming in polluted waters. Some live out their lives in the depths of the sea, never even knowing about the world above them. It's got to be a harsh way to live.

Eliot has always felt drawn to octomaids. Out of all the races, he finds them the most beautiful. Maybe because they are so alien to him, or maybe because they are more animalistic than other species. Or perhaps it's because he thinks they don't get enough love in their lives and fairies are instinctually driven to bring love into the lives of those who need it most.

CHAPTER SEVEN

"It's positive," Oona says, coming out of the bathroom with the pregnancy test in her hand.

She didn't bother showering off after getting back from the store, and her tentacles are still coated in black dirt and asphalt residue a centimeter thick from crawling three miles from where she ditched Avia's car. Eliot has a look of panic on his face, even more distressed than Oona. She holds up the test like it's not even a surprise to her.

"Are you serious?" he asks, taking the test from her to see the proof for himself.

"I guess the fairy tests do work on octomaids," she says. "I got another test to try later, but with what you said about your kind I doubt it's a false positive."

Eliot just holds the test in his hands, staring at it incredulously. He can't believe he did this to her. He was hoping the test would be negative so that he'd feel better about himself, but this only makes him want to die.

He looks at her and bursts into tears. Fairies are known to cry easily, but Eliot's always been able to hold back from exploding with emotion. This time he just can't help himself. He's responsible for killing someone he cares deeply about. There's nothing else he can do but let his emotions pour out.

"But..." he tries speaking, staring at the test, wiping tears away. "But there's got to be something we can still do. Maybe a doctor will know how to stop it."

Oona goes to him and pats his shoulder with a tentacle, trying to comfort him even though she's the one who is going to die.

"It's okay." She places her hand on the top of his head and ruffles up his pink hair, petting him like he's a child who's lost a toy. "Don't be sad. You're going to be a father."

He looks up at her. "But you're going to die because of me."

She shakes her head. "Most octomaids don't live as long as I have, so I'm not upset. It's just my time. It was going to happen soon anyway, whether I wanted it to or not. If it wasn't you, it would have been someone else."

"How can you just accept it so easily?"

Oona shrugs. "We're programmed that way. It's instinctual. In all honesty, it couldn't have happened at a better time."

Eliot wipes his tears. "What do you mean by that?"

"Everyone is going to know what happened to Niko soon, if they haven't already. Shino Kaji is going to want my head for that and Madam Nuri will make sure he gets it. They'll never find me if I return to the ocean. It's too vast, even for their reach. I'll be able to escape them, give birth to my offspring, and complete my lifecycle."

Eliot gets upset by her matter-of-fact tone. He can't imagine she'd actually be happy with that outcome. "But that's not what you really want. You're not ready to die. You want to live. You said so. We have to find another way."

She shakes her head. "You're not of my kind. You wouldn't understand. This is the right outcome." She pulls away from him, taking the pregnancy test from his fingers and placing it in the trash bin. "If you're concerned about yourself, you should know this is ideal for you as well. With me out of the picture, they'll never be able to track you down. You could go home now and be completely in the clear. Nobody would ever find you."

Eliot is almost angered by her words. "I'm not going anywhere.

I want us both to live. Besides, why would I be in the clear? Your friend Avia saw me. People at the Snake Pit know me. I'm not safe even if you disappeared."

"That's not how it works," Oona says. "They don't care about you. You're not connected. If I disappear, Madam Nuri will be held responsible for it, not you. She will have to go to war with the Sylphs or give up a large chunk of her business to appease them. Either way, they won't care about you. They have no idea you did the killing. They would never think you were capable of it. Everyone will be certain that I killed Niko to stop him from raping you. You're just a victim, a witness at best. You'll be fine."

Eliot turns from her, trying not to cry any more. He feels like such a piece of shit. Everything that happened to Oona was his fault, from Niko to the pregnancy. She wouldn't have to deal with any of this if he wasn't involved.

"But how am I supposed to just let you die?" he asks.

"You need to just let it go."

She slithers up behind him, hovering over him. When she places her hands on Eliot's shoulders to admire her work in his skin, all the distress fades from his body.

"But there's one thing that you can do as a favor to me," she says.

Eliot looks at her through a mirror on the wall. "What's that?"

"Your tattoos," she says. "Let me finish them. Give me a few days and I can complete my work. I don't mind dying if I know that I'll be leaving behind something that I'm proud of."

Eliot turns to her. "You're proud of my tattoos?"

She looks at him with her deep black eyes. Eliot can almost see love in them, even if it is just love for the art on his skin.

"They are my best work," she says. "I don't mind dying as long as my art lives on your body."

She rubs a tentacle down Eliot's tattooed arm and pushes him against the wall. His heart races. He thinks she's about to kiss him, but she just stares at the tattoos on his skin, making love to him with her eyes.

No matter what Eliot says, Oona has already made up her mind. All she wants to do is finish tattooing his skin. She spends hours staring at his naked body, imagining what designs she can put in the remaining spaces of flesh. Because it's the last piece she will ever complete, she wants it to be perfect.

"Are you sure you can finish in just a few days?" Eliot asks. "There's still a lot of skin left. It could take weeks, even if you did nothing but tattoo me day and night."

She can tattoo anything on him anywhere she wants for as long as she likes and he won't complain. There's nothing he won't do to make her happy, not after what he's done to her. But he feels awkward just lying there, every inch of his naked body subjected to her silent scrutiny. So his inquiry is really just an excuse to break up the silence with some conversation.

"I won't tattoo every inch of your body," she says, not taking her eyes off of him. "The negative space is where a full body piece really shines. It's not just the tattoos but the area that's not tattooed that really makes a great work. Most tattooists don't get the opportunity to use a complete body as their canvas. Too many clients already have some terrible tattoos that ruin the full piece. I was lucky that I found you when I did."

Her words make Eliot happy. There's nothing that pleases him more than when Oona sees him as her canvas. The first time she put her ink into his skin, he knew it was his destiny to be the carrier of her artwork. He'd never let anyone else corrupt it with a lesser tattoo.

"No matter what happens," she says, "I plan to leave my mark on the world. You're going to be the vessel that keeps my work alive."

Eliot nods. He can't be happier to do this for her.

As she begins tattooing him, Eliot loves the pain more than he's ever loved it before. He's always seen himself as her canvas, as her living work of art, but she's never admitted that she feels the same way about him. It fills him with pride and purpose. It gives him a reason to be alive.

He lets her do whatever she wants to his body. Even when he gets an erection, and has no washcloth to cover it up, he doesn't recoil from her needle. She inks his thighs with such intensity that she probably doesn't even notice the rest of his body. She's more committed to the piece than Eliot's ever seen, putting in more of her soul than Eliot ever thought possible. He's never witnessed so much passion in Oona, or any artist. It's the kind of passion you only see from someone who doesn't have very much life left, who is pouring everything they have into their creation.

A moan escapes Eliot's lips unconsciously and he isn't sure if it's a response to the pain of the needle or brought on by the ecstasy of seeing such beautiful artwork forming on his body. Oona doesn't cover up her art as she works, so he can see every line as it is carved into his skin. It's an intimate, powerful, ecstatic experience for him. He loves every second of it.

When she finishes for the night, he can't stop looking at the images. She's always tattooed designs in his flesh that resembled aquatic creatures, from fish to eels to crabs to mollusks, but she's never tattooed octopus tentacles on him before. But now on both of his thighs, she has created two bundles of tentacles that coil into a surreal mass which wraps around his legs, as though her art is hugging his limbs.

"It's beautiful," he says. "They might be my favorite pieces."

"It's all one piece," she says.

When his eyes look up they meet hers, she's leaning into him, staring deeply. He can tell she's turned on. He didn't even release any pheromones while she worked as he normally would, but she still seems like she wants him. The act of tattooing him has gotten her in the mood.

She kisses him and his wings twitch in excitement. Her lips are so big and her tongue is so thick and gooey that he can't help but give in.

Though, when she grabs his penis, he pulls back. "What are you doing?"

"What do you think?" she says, then continues to kiss him.

He pushes her back. "We can't. It's not safe."

She snickers, almost with annoyance. "What do you mean? I'm already pregnant. If I'm going to die I might as well have as much sex as I can before I return to the ocean." She sucks on his lip, just for a second. "It's how my kind does it. We spend our whole lives trying to be celibate until the moment that we find a mate, then we fuck ourselves blind, making up for a lifetime of sexual repression before we die."

But as she wraps her tentacles around him, he can't help but feel uncomfortable. It doesn't feel right.

"What if you're not really pregnant?" he asks. "If the test is wrong then we shouldn't do it again. It will only make it more dangerous."

She doesn't let go of his penis, stroking it with her hand as her tentacles curl around his lower body.

"We don't have to if you don't want to," she says, but she doesn't say this with understanding. She says it with resentment, as though she'll be pissed if he refuses her.

"No, I want to," he says, knowing that he's incapable of saying anything else. He's responsible for impregnating her, so he owes it to her to let her have her way. He has to let her take out her sexual urges on him. But he also knows there's no way back once he gives in. If the pregnancy test was wrong she'll surely get pregnant if they have sex again.

She slithers on top of him and looks down at his little body. She doesn't do anything for a while after that, just stares at him, squeezing him with her octopus legs.

"I never thought I'd end up with a guy who looks like you," she tells him. "I never thought I'd mate with a fairy."

She leans in and kisses his neck and then lays her head above his shoulder onto his wing.

"You're so small and pretty," she says. "Prettier than me."

Eliot shakes his head. "No one's prettier than you."

The second he says this she pulls his face to her lips and kisses him deeply. Then she wraps him up in her body and fucks the hell out him until there's glitter all over the room.

Eliot is still in love with Oona, but something about their lovemaking feels different this time. Last night it was like an erotic dream where he couldn't believe it was really happening. But this time it feels too real, too much like other women he's slept with. He wonders if the reason he was so interested in Oona was because she never showed any interest in him sexually. Because her survival depended on avoiding sex, her behavior makes quite a bit of sense to him now. But now that she has nothing left to lose, she is acting like every other woman he's ever known.

Although he'd never admit it to anyone, Eliot's been sexually assaulted on more than a few occasions. Sometimes by men, but more commonly by women. Women of most races are so much larger than him, even human and elven women, that he has no chance of fighting back. He's never known how to process when he's raped by a woman. The vast majority of people don't acknowledge women rapists are even a possibility, so he's never felt comfortable reporting any of his attackers. Most of the women who assaulted him probably wouldn't even see it as rape. They don't understand that fairies are sensitive to even the slightest touch, just having their wings caressed or their ears blown on stimulates a biological sexual response. And they think that just because he has an erection, he is consenting to have sex with them, no matter what he says to the contrary. He blames himself for not being clear enough with the words he chooses, not having a firm enough tone in his voice. But the idea of being too resistant always filled him with fear, like they might get angry and violent if he told them he didn't want them. He always thought it would be easier to just give in, let them finish and be done with it, a part of him still wanting them to like him despite the fact that he wanted nothing more than to get away from them. It's something fairies, regardless of gender, always have to deal with, even more than other races.

The way Oona forces him to make love to her reminds him of these encounters. Maybe it's the way she sticks him inside of her without asking permission. Maybe it's the way she ignores his cries when she shoves a tentacle up his ass or refuses to let go when she crumples his wings with her talon-like fingernails. Or maybe it's because she only sees the tattoos on his body when she fucks him, not even looking him in the eyes, just licking her art in his skin until she climaxes against him.

Nevertheless, he can't help but love her, no matter how it makes him feel. He wants her to enjoy herself, even if it hurts him, even if it makes him feel small. So long as she stays with him for as long as she possibly can. There's a part of Eliot that feels he deserves it anyway, especially after what he did to her. He should be lucky she wants to have anything to do with him at all. But no matter how much he loves her, no matter how much he deserves it, he still can't help but be reminded of all those past relationships where he was treated so badly and made to feel like less of a person.

For a moment, he starts to wonder if he really should trust Oona with his heart, someone who might just see him as another piece of fairy meat. But after she finishes coming against him, stops spraying him with her ink and strangling him with her tentacles, she looks at him with the most beautiful black eyes and smiles at him in such a powerful way that it completely wipes all of his worries and doubts right out of his mind.

She wraps herself around him in a loving embrace and he just cries with happiness, drenching her shoulder with his tears. There's not even any words between them. There is no need for words. The way she holds him, pulling him to her body as though she wants nothing more than to fill him with her love, means everything to him. He's sure she's not like all the others. She can't be. Not her.

Oona smooths out the damage she did to his wings, caresses the black eye she created above his cheek, and licks his tears right out of his eyeball. He shakes away all the bad memories of his past relationships and realizes he wants nothing more than to be with the woman holding him in her arms. He wants to spend the rest of his life with her. He wants her to live forever.

CHAPTER EIGHT

Oona tattoos Eliot every day and makes love to him every night until she finally finishes her design. She has Eliot turn around slowly in a circle, standing naked in the middle of the room, as she makes sure everything is perfect. Eliot feels odd as a living work of art, trying to live up to the standards of his artist. But no matter how much she stares at him, no matter how much of his body is covered in her designs, she never seems to be done.

"I think it looks great," Eliot says, looking at himself in the mirror.

She has tattooed his legs and ass, all of his back and torso. She's even tattooed his penis in such a way that it blends into the rest of his body. He was worried that his penis would stick out, either designed to look like a floppy little fish or be the only untattooed bit of flesh in the area, but instead she did it in such a way that his penis just disappears into the rest of the art, making it so that you focus more on the tattoos, even when it's erect. It's almost as if she's neutered him, made his penis invisible and irrelevant, but he doesn't mind so much. It makes it so that he's not so uncomfortable to stand in the nude around other people.

"I don't think I'm done yet," she says. "Let me touch up some of the old pieces and maybe I'll figure out what's wrong."

This is the fifth time she's done this. Eliot isn't sure if she isn't happy with the completed work or if she doesn't want their time together to end. He deeply wishes it was the latter. They have extended their hotel stay for twice what they were imagining they would. And because Oona plans to go to the ocean after this, and the fact that there's no way anyone can trace her to this hotel room, she's not in any hurry.

For the past two days, she's spent more time in bed with him than she has tattooing him, like she's more interested in their budding relationship than she is in finishing her art. It's almost too much for his little fairy body to handle, sometimes painful or damaging to his fragile bones. She presses against him, her three hearts pounding in her chest so loudly that Eliot can feel them in his own skin, and he can tell that she's saying that she loves him even though she hasn't expressed it in words.

He wants their time together to last forever, but when Oona decides she'd rather spend all day in bed with him than tattoo him at all, he knows that her artwork is finished, she just hasn't told him yet. Even though he's sick of eating crap from the vending machines and the convenience store across the street, and he's sick of sleeping in the rotten fish bed sheets that Oona won't let housekeeping come in to change, he could stay in this room forever with her if he was able to. But he knows that his time with her is almost at its end.

It's the ninth day in the room and Eliot can tell that it will be the day they say goodbye. Oona has Eliot pose for her for hours while she drinks cheap wine, smokes cigarettes and admires her completed work of art for as long as she can.

"You're so beautiful…" she says in a calm voice, almost too quiet for him to hear. "The most beautiful thing I've ever created."

"What was that?" Eliot asks, flickering his wings and hovering in a slow circle to display every angle of his body.

"I was mentioning how proud I am of you," she says. "You're my masterpiece. My ink… My artwork… embedded into your skin."

She takes a drink and pauses for a moment, eyeballing him. Then she asks, "How long do fairies live?"

Eliot stops moving. He lowers his arms and looks at her.

"We typically live for three hundred years," he says.

Oona smiles at his words. "Promise me you'll live that long. It would make me happy to know my art will live ten times my lifespan."

"These days fairies often die young," Eliot says. "We die in captivity or from drug overdoses. Suicide is also common. Some people kill us for sport or feed us to predators. I haven't heard of too many living past seventy in recent years."

Oona gets annoyed by his words. "I don't care about that. I want you to live that long. I want you to survive. Can you promise me that you'll survive for three hundred years? Will you keep my work alive that long?"

When she says this, Eliot observes the seriousness in her eyes. It's the look of a dying woman with one final wish. Eliot won't ruin it for her.

He looks her straight in the eyes, fluffing his wings behind his back, and tells her, "Yes, I will survive. I won't kill myself. I won't let anyone kill me. I won't touch drugs or anything that will give me cancer. I won't risk my life needlessly for anyone or anything. I will stay healthy so that I live as long as I possibly can. I will be your living work of art and I will make sure the whole world sees me."

After he says this, Oona just nods and smiles at him. Her big black eyes widen, become oily as if she's about to cry. Although Eliot has been telling her that he loves her for days now, she's never acknowledged his words. It isn't until he said this that she appears to realize he truly does love her. She hugs him closer than she probably has ever hugged anyone before.

"You better," she tells him, squeezing him so tightly with

her tentacles that she nearly rips his wings off. "If you don't I'll make sure our babies track you down the second they come out of the ocean and eat you alive."

Despite her words, Eliot can't help but smile and hug her back. It's the closest he's ever felt to another living being in his life.

Eliot knows it's time. Oona's about to say goodbye. She's all dressed, telling him that she wants to go to the store to get something, but the look in her eyes says that she isn't planning on coming back. Before she leaves the room, she looks back at Eliot. He stands there in his underwear, his tattoos are mostly healed and are a perfect shade of black and gray.

"Fairies are known to be the sexiest race on the planet, but I think I succeeded in making you the sexiest fairy of them all," she says.

He blushes at her. Before she leaves, he goes to kiss her. He won't let her leave him without saying goodbye. Even though he wants her to go the way she wants—if she wants to sneak away he'll give her that—he won't let her go without a last kiss.

"You don't know how much you've saved me," he tells her. "Thank you for giving me a reason to live."

Then he kisses her with all the emotions a fairy can give another person, which is far more than any race is accustomed to feeling, far more than Oona was expecting. As his lips weave into hers, she almost melts to the floor. He explodes his love into her body, so much that they almost see bright pink colors emanating between them. It's so overpowering that for the first time Oona feels small compared to him, despite being more than twice his size.

When he finishes kissing her, her tentacles ooze with mucus

and slide toward the floor, lowering her to his height. She gazes into his eyes as though she wants to rip off her clothes and make love to him again. But then she calms down, releasing the desire. She stands up straight and recomposes herself.

"I'll be back soon," she says.

Her voice doesn't even try to pretend that her words aren't a lie. She bows at him and turns away. Then she opens the door and is hit in the face with a spike-knuckled fist.

When Oona collapses on the ground, Eliot leaps into the air, fluttering his wings so fast that they make a loud buzzing sound. Three large lizard men enter the room. They grab Oona by a tentacle and drag her deeper inside, then throw her over the bed. Eliot recognizes one of them as a bouncer at the Snake Pit strip club, the one who helped him when he was being harassed by Niko the last night he was there. The man doesn't look nearly as nice as he did then. He looks more like a deranged thug who could pound them into a bloody pulp within seconds if he wanted to.

An old dragon lady steps into the room and closes the door behind them. She walks elegantly, wearing a long golden dress, her wrinkled scales show that she's lived for generations yet without signs of anger or stress. She doesn't acknowledge Eliot fluttering in the air above them, her eyes focused on the octomaid who still looks wobbly from the punch in her face.

"Madam Nuri..." Oona says, trying to get over her spinning head. "How the hell did you find me?"

The old lady sneers at her, looking her up and down.

"You think you could hide from me forever?" the old lady asks. "After your old frog friend came to me, begging me to get her out of Marius' clutches in exchange for information, it didn't take too long to find her vehicle you were driving.

After that, all I had to do was ask around about any octomaids seen in the area. You were stupid to stay on this side of town. Nobody forgets seeing an octopus in this neighborhood. You should have stayed in Naiad territory, at least then nobody would have paid you an ounce of attention."

Oona looks away. She knew it was careless. She only planned to stay for three days. That was the most that would have been feasible, but once she realized she was pregnant she didn't want to leave. She wanted to finish her artwork. She wanted to make love to Eliot. She didn't want to let go of her life on the surface so easily. But if she had left just a day, maybe even an hour earlier, she might have made it.

Madam Nuri paces across the carpet, examining the state of her old subordinate. "So this is where you've been for the past week, in this filthy love nest?" She sees the condition of the black sheets, covered in glitter and rotten fish stench. "It's disgusting."

Oona slithers upright, trying to stand on her tentacles. She has a look of panic in her eyes, something Eliot never thought he'd see. She opens her mouth to speak but can't think of anything to say.

Madam Nuri looks over at Eliot and then back at the octomaid. "All this over a fucking fairy? Are you serious, Oona? The Demon of Grub Town turns her back on her family for a little twink. What the hell's wrong with you?"

Oona looks at Eliot and back at her boss. "Leave him out of this. He had nothing to do with it."

Madam Nuri just sighs and steps closer to Oona. "You disappoint me, girl. I always treated you like a daughter. All the strings I pulled to get you out of Marius' clutches. And even when you didn't want to be my enforcer and focus on your little hobby, I did all I could to accommodate you. I never asked for anything. But because of you I'm on my knees, groveling to that elf bastard. Do you know how far you've set me back?"

Oona takes a deep breath. "I'm sorry, Mom. I fucked up.

But I can make it right. I promise."

Eliot never thought he'd see Oona in such a pitiable state. She looks like a child terrified of her abusive mother.

"I know you can make it right, Daughter," Madam Nuri says. "After I hand you over to Shino, you'll solve this whole mess you've made."

"It wasn't her fault!" Eliot cries. "I'm the one who killed Niko. Give me to Shino Kaji instead."

Oona glares at him, telling him to shut the fuck up with her eyes.

"Why is this twink speaking to me?" the dragon lady asks, not even looking in Eliot's direction.

"I'm sorry, he doesn't understand," Oona says.

"If he speaks again I'll swat him like a fly," says Madam Nuri. "The cleaning staff will be scrubbing his guts off the wall for days."

"I'll go with you if you leave him alone," Oona tells her, a tone of desperation in her voice.

Eliot wishes she would save herself. He's not afraid to face the boss of the elf yakuza. He has sentient blood. He could kill all of the elves the second he came into contact with them. Even if they shot him, he'd rip them to shreds with his dying breath. If only Oona would have acknowledged that he was the one to kill the boss's son, she might have been let free to go to the ocean to give birth. He has a better chance of surviving than she does. Trying to protect him is just foolish.

"I already have plans for him," says Madam Nuri. "He doesn't concern you anymore."

"I'm not going to go quietly unless you promise he'll be okay," Oona says.

Madam Nuri sneers at her adopted daughter. She says, "You're not in a position to bargain for anything."

Oona looks up at Eliot and then over at her boss. The second she leaps into the air, her tentacles reaching for the dragon lady's throat, two of the lizard men grab her and wrestle her to the ground. Despite her enormous size, they are able to toss her like she weighs nothing. Her tentacles wrap around their arms and legs, trying to get to their throats, as she screams at them.

When Eliot sees her life is in danger, he rips off the bandage on his arm and tries to reopen his wound with his teeth, trying to release his sentient blood to save her. But before he can even get a drop of blood from his body, the third lizard man grabs him by the leg and throws him against the wall. He flies headfirst. He barely even opens his mouth to cry out as his skull makes contact with the bricks and everything goes black.

CHAPTER
NINE

"I think he's waking up."

"Are you sure? He still looks out to me."

"I saw his eyelids twitch."

"He's been out for a long time."

"Croco must have hit him pretty hard."

"I hope he doesn't have brain damage."

"He might. Fairies are supposed to be pretty fragile."

"We should try to wake him up again."

"We're not in any rush. Let him sleep."

"But I'm sick of waiting around. Besides, he might have a concussion. You're not supposed to sleep if you have a concussion."

"Shake him then. See if it works."

"Wake up, Eliot."

"Wake up, Sleepy Head."

Eliot opens his eyes to see Tiki and Taka hovering over him, shoving him with their scaly fingers. Their long red hair dangles in his face. Their tall fake eyelashes blink at him. Their lips curl into smiles.

"Oh, he's awake!" Taka cries.

"Hi, fairy friend," Tiki says, waving at him right in his face. "Are you feeling alright? How's your head?"

"I feel stiff," Eliot says, rubbing the bump on the back of his skull. "I can't move."

The second he says this, he realizes he can't move because

their snake bodies are wrapped around him, holding him inside of a tight warm knot.

"Oh, you poor thing," Taka says. Her tail squeezes tighter around him.

Tiki pets his pink hair. "Croco is such a big meanie for hurting you like that."

Eliot looks around. He's still in his underwear, lying on the ground of a small room. The walls and floor are all tiled, like a bathroom. There's a toilet in the corner designed for snakes. A shower head is in the center of the room, hanging from the high ceiling, as though the place is meant for washing off large reptilians. A bench is attached to the wall. There's no windows or even air vents. The only door is heavy duty, probably reinforced with iron. It doesn't look like it opens from this side. There isn't a handle. It doesn't take him long to realize that he's in some kind of lamia prison cell.

"Where am I?" he asks, trying to sit up.

"We don't know," Taka says. "It's a secret place. They wouldn't tell us where."

Tiki explains, "Madam Nuri forced us to wear blindfolds before we came here, so we could be anywhere."

Taka looks around the cell. "We took a lot of stairs down, so we're definitely underground. In some basement of one of the family's businesses."

"I smelled blood," Tiki says. "I think it's a slaughterhouse."

Taka shakes her head. "No, I think it's a restaurant. On our way downstairs, I heard dishwashers and someone complaining about being almost out of lobster."

Tiki shrugs. "Either way, they wouldn't tell us anything. They seemed really mad when we asked."

Eliot feels bad for the twins. He worries that he got them involved in all of this for being his friends, terrified that he got them both imprisoned with him because of what he did to Niko Kaji. The idea that they will likely share his fate, whatever that might be, fills him with guilt. But what worries him even more than what will become of the three of them is what happened to the woman he loves.

"Where's Oona?" he asks. "Have you seen her?"

They give him cute frowns.

"Oh, I'm so sorry, Eliot," Tiki says, almost about to cry as she looks him in the eyes.

"She's in trouble with Madam Nuri," Taka says. "They said she did some very bad things and is going to be punished."

"She was taken to the elves," Tiki says. "I don't think she's going to make it."

When they see the look of anguish on Eliot's face, it brings tears to their eyes.

"Ohhh, poor Eliot," Tiki says. "You loved her so much, didn't you?"

"It's so sad I want to cry," Taka says.

They pet him and squeeze him with their tails, trying to make him feel better. But he's not ready to give up on her. He has to find a way out of this cell. He's not sure what a simple fairy can do against the elf yakuza, even one with sentient blood, but he can't just let her die. There's got to be something he can do.

"I have to save her," Eliot says. He tries to get up, but he's too coiled up to move. The twins only squeeze tighter, making sure he doesn't get away, as though trying to calm him with their loving embrace.

Taka hushes him. "You have to forget about her."

Tiki strokes his hair. "There's nothing you can do."

Eliot tries to pull himself from their grasp. "There's a lot we can do. You have to trust me. If we just get a guard to open the door, I can—"

Before Eliot can wiggle himself free, Taka squeezes him so forcefully that all the air gushes out of his lungs and he can't speak or breathe.

"Just calm down…" Taka says. She releases her grip a little to let him get some air. "Everything isn't so bad. You still have us."

"We're here for you," Tiki says, her tongue flickers from her lips.

Eliot takes deep breaths. He can feel the warmth emanating from Taka's scales as she's wrapped around him, her heartbeat pulsing against his stomach. Despite the situation, he's happy to be with his friends. They always know how to cheer him up, even when everything is at its worst. Though he feels that he might have gotten them into trouble, he's glad to be in their company.

"We can escape if we work together," he tells them.

But they just ignore his words, acting as flighty and distracted as usual.

Taka pinches the edge of his wing and rubs it between her fingers.

"You don't know how much we fought to be here with you," she says.

Tiki rubs his tattooed arm up and down and says, "When we heard that Madam Nuri was going to have you killed, we begged her so much to not go through with it. We thought it would be such a waste."

Eliot is confused by their words. "What do you mean? You convinced her not to kill me?"

"Well..." Tiki's eyes roll to the side, trying to keep the smile off her face. "No, not exactly."

Taka adds, "She was going to let the elves kill you. They were going to make you suffer and you would've died in a horrible painful way. But we begged her to let us have you instead."

When they look deep into his eyes, he's beginning to understand what they're talking about.

"You mean..." he begins.

"You've been such a good friend to us," Tiki says, rubbing her index finger down his chest. "If you have to die we want to make sure it's a pleasurable experience for you. We want you to die happy."

Eliot looks back and forth at the red racer twins. He can't

believe what they're implying.

Taka goes right out and says it, "We're going to eat you." Her long snake tongue licks her lips after she says this, staring deep into Eliot's eyes.

Tiki adds, "Madam Nuri was mad when we asked her, but we couldn't just let you die in a horrible way. You're our little fairy friend. We begged her to let us eat you. She agreed as long as we promised to do other work for her from now on, but we don't care what we have to do as long as we can make you feel good when you die."

Taka points to a camera in the corner of the ceiling that Eliot hadn't noticed before. "They're going to record it and send it to the elves. That was the only condition they had for letting us go through with it. As long as they can see you die, everything will be alright."

"It'll all be okay," Tiki says.

"We'll make sure it's fun for you," Taka says.

When they finish speaking and Eliot looks up at their bright smiling faces, he doesn't know what to think about them. He wonders if they're completely insane. A part of him thinks that in their own ridiculous way they think they're actually doing him a favor. It's like they believe he will be appreciative that they get to murder him. Even though they have clients who literally would give their lives to experience being swallowed alive by lamias, Eliot just sees it as a horrific way to die. He can't possibly think of it as anything he should be grateful for.

"Besides..." Taka says, her eyes glistening at him. "I've always wanted to see what a fairy tastes like."

"You're probably so yummy!" Tiki cries.

"This is going to be so good," Taka says. "You don't even have to pay for it. We're happy to eat you for free."

As Eliot recognizes the predatory looks in their eyes, he wonders if the red racer twins were ever friends with him in the first place. He wonders if they were just working on him the whole time, trying to seduce him a little every day, hoping to someday convince him to one day be their food. They knew he was good at saving up money for tattoos, so he surely would be able to get the money to pay for being swallowed, if only he had a desire to do so. It makes him wonder about the time they had him stay with them while they digested their previous clients. Perhaps they were just trying to introduce him to the fetish, get him turned on to the possibility that he could be a future meal.

Or maybe they really are just innocent. Maybe they've seen eating men as a sexual act, as an expression of love, for so long that they forgot how normal people are terrified by the idea. Maybe they really do think they're just being nice. Maybe calling him yummy is just their way of giving him a compliment, like how they've always said he had pretty wings and cute hair. Maybe they aren't the horrible people he's beginning to suspect they might be.

Eliot knows he's got to find a way out of his current situation. If they really care about him, the twins would help him find a way to escape. If only he can convince them that this isn't the only option, maybe they can work together to free themselves from the cell and then rescue Oona.

"I don't want you to eat me," he tells them, squirming in their grip. "You don't have to do this. Just let me go and we'll figure a way out of here."

They ignore him, staring at his body like he's just a delicious little snack to them. Taka's tongue flickers against his lower abdomen, sniffing at the sweat that perspires from his pores. Tiki rubs a hand down his chest and arms.

"Your tattoos are so hot," Tiki says, touching the designs in his skin. "Oona finished her work while you two went into hiding, didn't she? They look so amazing."

146

"So fancy…" Taka says. "I've always loved edible art."

"And they're made with octopus ink," Tiki adds. "Octopus ink is supposed to be really tasty."

Taka says, "I wonder if it will make him taste like seafood…"

They giggle to each other. He can't tell if they're serious or just teasing him. Their usual clients probably would get off on that kind of talk so they could just be doing it for his benefit. He hopes this isn't how they really feel.

"Please, listen to me," Eliot says, struggling against them. "We can escape if we work together."

The red racer twins are beginning to get annoyed by his resistance.

"You need to get into the spirit of things, Eliot," Tiki says. "This'll be fun for you if you just give in and enjoy it."

"Besides, there's no way out of the room," Taka says.

Tiki points at the snake toilet in the corner. "They're not going to open the door until they see us poop you out in there."

Eliot looks at the toilet in horror. He wonders if this room is designed for lamias to get rid of enemies of the reptile mafia. He imagines how many people have been eaten and shit out in that toilet. The pipes are probably coated in a thick residue made from the powdered bones of the dead.

Taka leans in close and whispers gently, "Don't let our enthusiasm frighten you. We've never eaten a fairy before. It's kind of exciting for us."

The twins pull off their bikini tops to show him their breasts. Their chests are incredibly pale, almost vampiric, with deep red nipples that match the color of their scales. Although lamias are known to be the most curvaceous of any species, perfect hourglass bodies with large breasts and even larger hips, the red racer twins are a little lacking in that department. Their breasts are a bit small compared to most lamias, their hips a bit narrow, but they are almost more beautiful because of it, their curves the perfect match for their body sizes. Eliot has seen them naked while dancing on stage many times before, but he's never seen their bodies up close. He's almost instantly hypnotized by their beauty.

They look him in the eyes and flicker their tongues at him. Then they pull off Eliot's underwear like they're removing the wrapper from a piece of candy. There's nothing he can do to stop them. His wings flicker against their tails. His antennae droop down on his forehead like the ears of a scared puppy dog.

Tiki tosses his underwear over her shoulder and admires the tattoo work on the area she just uncovered, sliding a finger up his inner thigh toward his penis. He becomes almost instantly erect, his body not able to control it despite the fear flooding through his mind.

When Tiki sees his erection, she smiles up at him. "There you go. I knew you'd like the idea of being eaten by us."

"He just needs to be properly motivated." Taka slithers up his body and rubs her breasts in his face, like she's giving him a lap dance with no music. Her breasts are incredibly silky and smooth, sending a calming sensation through his body. He can't help but close his eyes and enjoy the feeling. Her skin is covered in cocoa butter and a light dusting of baby powder, giving it the same silken texture as when she's working in the strip club.

The twins lift Eliot in the air and coil around his body, wrapping him up with their tails, weaving together until they are all in a vertical knot. He finds himself tight between their bodies. Tiki's breasts squished in his face, Taka's breasts in the back of his neck. He can hardly breathe as they smother him and crush his wings against their scales.

"He's so light and delicate," Taka says.

"He's probably not used to being handled so roughly," Tiki says.

The twins speak over Eliot's head, their faces inches away from each other. They rub themselves against him, squeezing him like constrictors. Their snake scales are smooth and firm against his naked skin. He can feel nothing but thick muscle beneath the scales. The girls are probably strong enough to bend metal bars with their tails.

Eliot feels a wetness gush against his erection. He realizes that his penis is pressed against Tiki's labia and it is causing her to become aroused. Her labia swells out of her scales as she rubs against him. She giggles to herself as she presses him closer to her entrance, but she doesn't pull him inside of her. She just rubs her vaginal lips against his penis, the scales scratching against his thighs as she squeezes him tighter.

"Please…" Eliot says, his words muffled in her soft cleavage.

But they interpret his words as a plea to continue, not to free him. Tiki's vagina envelops his penis, just for a moment, and then she lets it go. She has complete control of her labia, able to suck on him like the lips of a mouth.

"Loosen your grip on him for a moment," Tiki tells her sister.

Taka's tail releases from Eliot's body and Tiki lifts him higher, rubbing her labia down his body until it reaches his toes. She pulls him in feet first, sucking him in up to his ankle. Her vaginal walls tighten up against the balls of his feet, soaking him with thick warm saliva. Eliot squirms at the sensation.

When Taka realizes what is going on, she cries, "Hey! What are you doing?"

"I'm just tasting him," Tiki says, giggling.

"You said I'd be the one who gets to eat him!" Taka cries, pouting like a child whose toy was taken away.

Tiki pulls Eliot down to his knees, soaking him in her warmth.

"I won't go all the way," Tiki says.

"You better let me eat him. You promised."

The flesh inside of Tiki is not like that of a vagina. It's more like a mouth. He feels like his legs are wrapped up in a large gooey tongue.

Tiki squeals in delight. "Oh my god! He tastes so good.

He's so sweet and delicate, like eating a flower."

Eliot's skin is beginning to burn as Tiki's acidic juices get into the open wounds of his recent tattoos. It isn't enough to hurt him, but it makes him squirm, kicking his feet inside of her.

Taka places her chin on Eliot's shoulder, whispers in his ear, "It feels nice, doesn't it? Our lower mouths are lined with taste buds so that we can savor the flavor of our prey. We actually have a stronger sense of taste down there than in our upper mouths. Lamia tongues are used more for smelling than tasting."

Taka pushes him deeper into her sister, up to his thighs. As he feels more of Tiki's insides, he realizes that it really is like another mouth, but there's no teeth and the tongue is spread out across its inner walls. A lot of people think lamias eat their prey with their vaginas, but their reproductive organs are actually separate body parts, hidden within the lower mouth.

"I've never tasted anything like him," Tiki says, a smile widening on her lips. "He doesn't taste meaty and fatty like humans. His flesh is fruity and tender... like mangoes."

Tiki moans as she gulps him to his pelvis, sucking his ass and penis inside of her mouth. The head of his cock rubs against her clitoris, tickling her, and she laughs in delight at the sensation. She looks down at him with her tongue flapping between her lips.

"Okay, you've tasted him enough," Taka complains. "Spit him out. I want a turn."

"Let me fuck him for a while," Tiki says, giggling as she grinds against him. "His dick feels so nice. It's so gentle and willowy. It's like a girl's dick."

"Girls don't have dicks," Taka says in an annoyed tone.

"Yeah, but if girls did have dicks they'd feel like this. It's slender and feminine. It's so sweet."

Tiki grabs Eliot's ass through her snake scales and pushes him closer, sliding his penis up into her pussy. Eliot cringes at the feeling. It's not what he wants. Tiki's like a sister to him.

He's always thought she was pretty, but he never wanted to have sex with her. But when he tries to climb out of her, it only pushes his penis deeper inside. It's liked he's hooked in the mouth of a fish. He can only go up into her vagina or deeper down her throat.

"Tiki, don't..." he says, but his words are soft and quiet. He's not sure if she can hear. He's not sure if he even wants her to hear.

As Tiki moans at the pleasure, her sister unravels from them and backs away. Eliot's wings expand, stretching out the wrinkles from being crumpled against Taka's body. He flaps them rapidly, trying to fly out of the snake's mouth, but it only makes Tiki more excited. She cries out in ecstasy and squeals with glee. Her tail wags across the tile floor, swollen with his lower body, coiling with every thrust. Because he is not doing any of the work of fucking her, trying to resist, she has to use her hands to push his body up and down.

"Oh, he tastes so good..." Tiki cries as she fucks him. "I wish I could eat fairies every day."

As she makes love to him, the acids inside her get stronger, releasing more digestive fluids as he moves up and down in her throat. His flesh burns so much that he cries out. He feels like his lower body is being dissolved, like layers of skin are being melted away. Tiki squeezes the muscles in her snake body around Eliot, compressing him with so much pressure that he feels like his two legs are becoming one.

Tiki looks down at him and smiles. "Oh, you look so cute inside of me, Eliot." She rubs his arms and shoulders. "Your tattoos are so sexy. I want to eat you all up."

Taka glares at her, telling her that she better not even think about it. When Eliot looks over at her, he notices that she has her fingers inside of her lower mouth, masturbating at the spectacle. He's not sure if she's turned on by watching her sister eat another man or if she is just getting herself ready for her own turn.

Eliot looks back at Tiki and says, "You have to stop."

But Tiki is so overwhelmed that she closes her eyes, almost as though she's reaching orgasm. Then she looks at Eliot and puts her hands on his shoulder, shoving him deeper into her mouth.

She cries, "I'm sorry. I just have to eat him."

Taka freaks out. "What! You can't!"

Tiki continues pushing him deeper, his penis sliding out of her vagina as her lips crawl up his abdomen. "He's just so delicious. You have to let me have him."

"But I didn't even get to taste him yet!" Taka cries.

Tiki stuffs Eliot's wings into her mouth, squishing them in like tissue paper in a Christmas present. "Please let me do this. I can't help myself. I'll make it up to you later, I promise."

"You're such a selfish pig!" Taka yells, coiling up into an angry ball. But as she takes a couple deep breaths, she calms down and says, "Fine... But you owe me big time for this."

Tiki's face lights up with excitement. She smiles down at Eliot. "Did you hear that, fairy friend? I get to be the one who eats you. Aren't you happy?" She giggles at him. "You wanted me to be the one to eat you anyway, didn't you? I've always been your favorite."

"I don't want either of you to eat me!" Eliot cries.

Tiki gives him a sad face and says, "Please let me eat you, Eliot. You taste so good. It would make me so happy."

She's trying to cute him into being submissive, but he's not going to fall for it. He promised Oona that he would survive for her. He can't let her artwork be digested in the body of a snake woman. He's responsible for more than just himself now, he's responsible for preserving her masterpiece. Even if he can't save her life, he knows that he has to save her art.

"If you eat me you'll die," he tells Tiki. "I have sentient blood." He puts his wrist to his mouth, opening his jaws as if ready to bite into his wound and release the parasite. "I don't want to, but I will kill you if you don't stop."

He's not sure if Tiki even knows about what sentient blood would do to her if he released it from his body. Taka's eyes light up with concern, but her sister doesn't seem fazed by the information. She quickly grabs Eliot's wrist away from his mouth and tucks his hands inside of her mouth, squeezing them so that he can no longer move.

"Don't fight it, Eliot," she tells him. "There's nothing you can do to stop this. Just be quiet and let me eat you."

"You don't understand," Eliot says, tears forming in his eyes as he's drawn deeper into her body. "Eating me will kill you. If you try to digest me the blood will escape from my body and tear you to shreds from the inside out. I don't want that to happen. I don't want you to die."

Tiki gives him a cute frown. "Oh, it's so cute you're worried about me. You really are a sweety. I'm still going to eat you, though. You just taste too good to stop now."

Then she leans back and sucks him down, her lower mouth pulling him down on its own, making audible gulping sounds as she slurps him up. She moans out loud and arches her back as his face rubs against her clitoris on his way down. When she swallows him up completely, her snake body squeezes him tightly. He wriggles inside of her, struggling to get back out, but her mouth closes tightly over his wings, the tips still sticking out. As he continues down her throat, he pulls his hand up toward his mouth. But the pressure becomes more intense. Tiki's muscles squeeze against him, crushing him. He hears a popping in his joints and bones as her body compresses him with tremendous force.

If he goes any deeper her muscles will constrict him into a tiny string of meat. He gets his wrist to his mouth as all of the air is crushed from his lungs.

He wheezes out the words, "I'm sorry, Tiki."

And then bites deep into his wrist.

His blood gushes out and becomes steel blades that cut through Tiki's abdomen. The pressure releases and he's able to breathe as her snake body is sliced open and he spills out onto the floor.

Eliot coughs and gags, holding the pain in his body. He feels like he has broken ribs and dislocated knees. Tiki only has a split second to scream as the metal parasite whips through the air, cutting the rest of her to pieces. When he gets to his knees and looks over at her remains, she appears to have been put through a meat slicer. He hardly recognizes the cheerful lamia that he used to like so much.

Taka backs away, slithering to the corner of the room, her eyes in shock at the silver blades coming from Eliot's body.

"How could you do that to Tiki?" she yells at him. "She was your friend. She just wanted to make you happy."

Eliot coughs Tiki's blood onto the floor and looks over at the remaining twin.

"I'm sorry..." he says. "I told her not to do it."

"She liked you so much!" Taka cries.

The lamia slithers closer, trying to get in his face and chastise him for murdering her twin. But as she gets within reach of the metal blood, Eliot waves his hands at her.

"Stay back!" he cries.

But it's too late. Once she gets within range, the blood spreads out into a dozen quills of metal and pierces through her body, impaling her skull and chest in ten different places. She dies before she hits the ground.

Eliot cries out loud when he sees what he's done to them. He's always loved Tiki and Taka so much, he can't believe he let this happen. He knows that they left him no choice, but he wishes there could have been another way. If only he could have convinced them to hold back. If only they understood what he would do to them if they forced him to defend himself.

The blood hovers in the air like a cloud of liquid metal,

constantly changing shape from blades to hooks to needles, ready to attack anyone who comes near.

Eliot looks up at the camera. He knows people are watching. Somebody is completely aware that he killed Tiki and Taka and that he is still alive. They also know that he's perfectly capable of defending himself.

CHAPTER TEN

It doesn't take long before a group of lizard men march down the stairs and pile into the hallway toward Eliot's prison cell. The second they burst through the door, Eliot's parasite shoots forward at them, forming into metal blades. But the lizard men are prepared to deal with him. They use the door as a shield, creating a barrier that the swords and spears of blood can't penetrate, holding their position as the liquid metal cuts and splats against their makeshift barricade.

The lizard men wait a second and then open the door a crack, firing blindly into the room. Eliot's blood is sprayed with bullets but the rounds just pass through the liquid and hit the wall behind him. Before they can take aim and fire on the fairy's position in the center of the room, Eliot leaps into the air, fluttering all the way to the ceiling to stay out of their line of fire. The bullets tear through the lamia corpses and shred the tiles on the walls into chunks of powder, but Eliot is high enough to remain untouched.

Eliot hovers in the air, becoming lightheaded without his blood in his body. If the parasite trying to protect him doesn't kill his attackers soon, the fairy will pass out and fall to the floor. The blood will have no choice but to return to his blood vessels and leave him defenseless and out cold. His skin is freezing. His wings become weak and can barely hold him up in the air. His eyesight gets blurry. He thinks he might have to pull his blood back in, just for a moment, even if it leaves him open to attack.

But his blood has a mind of its own and refuses to give up. It has intelligence and cunning. It knows how to kill no matter the circumstances. The liquid metal drops to the ground and oozes under the crack of the door. While the lizard men are spraying bullets into the room, the blood becomes spears of iron and impales them before they even know what's happening. Eliot just hears their screams and bodies being ripped apart as he descends to the floor. There's a final whimper as the last of them falls dead in the hallway. Then Eliot's blood pulls itself back into his arm and circulates through his bloodstream, bringing feeling back to his limbs, easing the pain in his head.

Weak in the knees as he pulls on his underwear and exits the prison cell. He grips his bloody wrist, pointing it outward like he's aiming a gun, ready to release a spray of sentient liquid metal at the first sign of danger. But there's no one else around. Just a pile of dead reptilians. Five of them. The hallway is quiet. It doesn't appear as though any other guards will be coming to stop him.

The hallway is desolate and colorless with cement floors and white plaster walls. It is filled with doors to prison cells the same as the one Eliot was kept in with Tiki and Taka. He can't see inside of the cells, nor hear any noises coming from within. He doesn't know if anyone is currently being held captive in any of them, but if there were he would like to set them free. He only opens a few doors. All three cells are empty but they seem to have gotten plenty of use in the recent past. One of them is coated in dried blood, as though somebody had been ripped apart by a wild animal.

He decides he doesn't have time to deal with any of the others. He's got to focus on finding Oona. If she is being held here it will be a simple task to rescue her, but Tiki and Taka told him she was being taken to the elves. It's going to be difficult to find Shino Kaji. He doesn't know much about the Sylphs apart from them being the biggest traffickers of fairies in the city. It's not going to be easy to track them down. It's going to be even harder getting to Oona without being captured. He'll surely be killed or sold into slavery, but he's got to take the risk. He can't just do nothing.

"I'm coming, Oona…" Eliot says.

His wings flitter and lift him off the ground. He flies through the hallway toward the stairs, his silver blood dripping from his wrist as he goes, forming a long trail across the cement floor. At the end of the hallway, he sees two signs pointing in different directions. One of them reads "Holding Cells" the other reads "Feeding Pens." He had been held in one of the feeding pens. He's not sure what kind of place this is, but he knows that it's not a place he wants to linger for long. There are cameras everywhere. He's surely being watched. The reptiles know he's escaped.

Not sure of the way out, he flies up the stairs and goes to the first door he can find. He bursts through, holding his wrist as though ready to attack anyone waiting to ambush him on the other side. But he doesn't find armed men geared up to stop him. He doesn't come across more pens or lamias or mafia thugs. Instead, he finds himself standing in the middle of an upscale restaurant.

Humans, elves, and dragonian customers are sitting at tables, eating their meals in a luxurious setting. The place is lavishly decorated in marble and red velvet curtains. Classical music is performed by a live string quartet. Everyone is dressed in tuxedoes and gowns. It is perhaps the fanciest restaurant

Eliot has ever seen, but there's something off about it. There are no windows, no noticeable exits. Despite the smiles and laughter of the guests, he can also hear whimpering and distant cries of agony.

Hovering in the middle of the room, Eliot noticeably stands out among the guests. Everyone in the room stops their boisterous conversations and looks over at him. The fairy flutters there in his underwear, tattoos covering him from head to toe, holding the silver blood dripping between his fingers. The guests snicker and point. The waiters pull out their phones to immediately report him, but he's not sure if it's to the police or to the lizard man thugs who were keeping him in the basement.

Before he makes a dash for it, something catches his eyes. Something is shifting and squirming on the closest dinner table, something desperate to attract his attention, and Eliot finally realizes just what is wrong with this restaurant. The people sit in their nice suits and colorful dresses, with their smug smiles and upturned noses, eating pieces of flesh that they shouldn't be legally allowed to consume. In the center of each of their tables, there lies a different woman that is being held against her will. All of them are women of the sea.

On one table, a naked mermaid is tied and gagged, lying on a large serving platter. The humans at her table are cutting off pieces of the fish part of her body and eating them cold and raw like sashimi. But she's still alive, looking over at Eliot with torment in her eyes. They seem to be enjoying the beautiful woman one piece at a time, trying to keep her alive as long as they can. Eliot's seen sushi displays served on the bodies of naked women before, but this takes that concept in a whole new atrocious direction.

On another table, a lobster woman lies dead and steamed as a group of elves dig into her tail, ripping out chunks of flesh and dipping it in a thick butter sauce. There are also crab girls and squid girls. Other tables farther back seem to be eating baked clam girls and soup made from the fins of shark maidens. Eliot sees it as cannibalism, but the customers are completely casual about it, as though it's just another high-end seafood restaurant to them.

If Madam Nuri is behind this, she's even worse of a person than he thought possible. All of these rich assholes are the scum of the earth as far as he's concerned. Eliot is completely appalled. He was already offended by how the upper classes treated merfolk, but turning them into livestock is something Eliot can never forgive. This could have been any of the mermaids he saw in Naiad territory. This could have been Lily. This could have been Oona. He wants every single one of these people to pay for what they've done.

The customers look at Eliot and smile, pointing at him like he might be available to be eaten as their dessert. None of them have fairies on their plates, but they might see him as a rare delicacy that they've been dying to experience.

When Eliot sees the suffering in the eyes of the meals who are still living, he can't help himself but want to save them or at least avenge them. He releases his hand from his wrist and lets his blood spill out. The looks on the customers' faces transform from smiles to dread as his sentient blood spirals into the air.

"Fucking animals…" he yells as his blood turns to spears of metal and is driven into the chests of the nearest patrons before they even know what's happening, coughing up chunks of raw fish as they die.

He doesn't have time to deal with every single one of them, but he plans to take out as many as he can as he makes his escape. He flies slowly through the room, allowing his blood to slice through the screaming diners, cutting them up in a spiral of blades. They cry out and try to escape, but his blood has a far enough reach to stab them no matter where they run, no matter which tables they try hiding beneath. A group of staff members, mostly waiters and musicians, try escaping through a door that must lead into the kitchen, but Eliot's blood forms into a scythe-like blade and cuts them in half just before they get through.

The blood avoids the women on the tables, maybe not seeing them as a threat. The mermaids take the opportunity to roll off of the tables and try to bite through their restraints. There's not enough time for Eliot to help them any further. He just keeps moving, unleashing his metal blood on the clientele, trying to look for an exit.

"Thank you," one of the mermaids says to him as he passes her by. She hides under a table, only a few bites taken out of her, one of the lucky ones. But the look of terror in her eyes slowly turns to wrath, licking her lips as she watches the fairy decapitate those who wanted to eat her. She slaps one of them across the knees with her fish tail as he tries to make his escape, slowing him down just long enough for him to receive a blade of silver across his throat. The rain of his blood trickling down on the mermaid's tail brings a satisfying smile across her face.

Eliot just nods at her as he passes, hoping that she'll be able to get out on her own, get herself home to safety and maybe even tell the authorities about this place, if there are any cops left who aren't on Madam Nuri's payroll.

The room is full of blood and body parts when Eliot gets to the other side of the restaurant. He follows a few survivors who got away from the initial onslaught, hoping that they'll eventually lead him to the exit. But before he can escape the building, a group of reptilian guards flood into the room and get in his way. One of them is Croco, the lizard man bouncer at the Snake Pit, the same one who punched him in the face back in the hotel room. This must be the guy who brought Eliot here, after he separated from Oona and Madam Nuri. He's the one who put him in the cell with Tiki and Taka, resulting in the deaths of his two friends.

When Eliot looks Croco in the eyes, he knows that he's the one he needs to talk to if he's ever going to find his way back to Oona. If anyone knows where Madam Nuri took her, he would.

The lizard men have looks of shock on their faces when they see Eliot's metal blood whipping in a spiral through the air around him. Eliot charges forward, flying at top speed directly at them. His blood cuts through the last of the restaurant customers, scattering their pieces across the walls and carpet. Eliot stops his assault and hovers in place the second they pull their guns and aim them at him.

Eliot pulls his blood back into his body as he lands in front of them. They don't dare shoot him. He's close enough to tear them all to pieces if a single bullet pierces his skin.

"If you move I rip you to shreds," Eliot tells them.

The lizard men freeze up, staring at the fairy's blood dripping through his fingers. For such large threatening men, they suddenly look like frightened kitty cats, wobbling at the knees. They must feel pathetic to be at the mercy of a tiny little fairy.

Eliot goes to Croco, "You know where Oona is. I need you to take me to her."

Croco shakes his head and speaks in a deep raspy lizard voice, "You're not going anywhere, insect."

But when Eliot holds his wrist closer, the lizard man cowers, recoiling back. He's seen what the blood can do. The place is filled with dead bodies. Even though he is armed, there's no way he can get out of the situation alive. None of them can. Shoot the fairy and his blood will be released into a storm of swirling blades.

"All you have to do is take me to her location," he says. "None of you have to die."

The lizard man looks at his friends and then looks into the fairy's eyes. "Nuri brought her to Shino Kaji. Even if I took you there, you wouldn't get out of there alive."

"I don't care," Eliot says.

Croco sneers and looks away, then he holds up his gun in defeat.

"She's probably already dead anyway," Croco says.

It looks like he's about to give in, surrender to Eliot's demands. But the second he turns around, a bullet pierces his skull and he falls to the ground. Eliot flies up into the air and backs away as the lizard men are showered with bullets from behind. They only get off two shots before they all crumple to the ground.

Eliot releases his blood, lets it fan out like a wide silver angel wing of razors. A group of shark men carrying submachine guns pile into the room, aiming them at the fairy. He holds his ground, waving his wing of razors in their direction.

"Stay back," he tells them.

They are obviously Naiads, but he has no idea what they're doing here. The shark men hold their ground, not as afraid of Eliot's blood as the lizard men were. It's as though they have no fear of dying whatsoever.

"Put your blood away, little butterfly," says a voice behind the shark men.

A large figure oozes through the crowd toward Eliot. When he comes into view, Eliot sees an octoman with thick gray tentacles slithering across the marble floor. He wears a long tan trench coat with a fluffy striped scarf. A brown top hat centers his head and a cane that could only be used as a fashion accessory is curled into one of his tentacles.

"We're not here to hurt you," he says, slithering closer, as close as he can without coming within range of his metal blood. "We just have a few questions we'd like to ask you concerning the whereabouts of my sister, Oona."

Eliot is thrown off guard by the octoman's words.

"You're Oona's brother?" Eliot asks.

The octopus man bows and dips his top hat. "My name is Marius. It's nice to meet you, my butterfly friend."

Eliot pulls his blood back into his body and watches as Marius slithers across the room, shifting through the blood of the dead elves and human restaurant customers, his attention directed toward the tables of half-eaten merfolk.

When he puts together what is going on in this place, Marius says, "I knew there was a reason I didn't like Madam Nuri." His voice doesn't change from its chipper tone, despite seeing his own kind splayed out as banquet fodder. "It's a pity we'll have to wipe her out for this. She was quite the business woman, once upon a time. You know, for a dragon."

The shark men move in and assist the mermaids struggling to free themselves from their serving platters. They gun down any remaining customers and waiters hiding under tables or behind the curtains, then move their attention to the kitchen staff hiding in the next room. Their cries for mercy last for only a moment as the shark men put bullets in their heads and toss their bodies away like trash. No matter how much the rich scumbags offer in payment, they all suffer the same fate. Unfortunately, only a few mermaids look like they'll be able to pull through. The rest have to be put out of their misery.

Eliot follows the octoman through the dining room, curious about who he really is. "Oona never said she had a brother in the Naiads."

Marius smiles. "Of course she wouldn't. We had a bit of a falling out some years ago. But we have history. We came up from the ocean depths together, came up in the Naiad family together. There's no one in the world I care for more than my dear sister."

"Does she feel the same way?" Eliot asks.

Oona said she'd rather die than rejoin the Naiads. She must not be too fond of her dear brother, despite what he's saying.

Marius snickers. "It doesn't matter how she feels. We're family and I'll do anything to get her back. I think it's about time she takes her rightful place by my side." He turns to Eliot. "You're her friend, aren't you? A little frog told me about a butterfly acquaintance of my sister who matches your description."

Eliot steps back as the octoman's tentacles slither in his direction, holding up his wrist as if ready to attack. "Oona is more than my friend. We're lovers."

When Marius hears this, he laughs at the fairy's preposterous statement. Eliot realizes how stupid he is for saying such a thing. He's not even sure Oona would call them lovers, despite all the times they spent in bed together.

"Sure you are, little butterfly," Marius says, amused by the fairy. "I can see her wanting to partake in a delicious little snack like you, but don't think she has any feelings for a mere insect. My sister is a cold-blooded killer. She cares for no one but herself. It's one of the reasons I love her so."

Eliot isn't sure he can believe the octopus. He doubts Marius knows much about his own sister, not the person she is now. She's been with Madam Nuri for years, most of it as a simple tattoo artist. She probably was only a child when she was last with the Naiad family.

"Oona cares about me," Eliot says. "And I care about her."

The octoman laughs again. "Of course I believe you, little butterfly. It's why you're still alive. I need your help finding her. One of my men saw you being stuffed in a trunk outside of a rundown motel and followed you here. He thought Oona would be here as well, but I suppose he was wrong, wasn't he?"

Eliot nods. "Madam Nuri brought her to Shino Kaji." He grinds his fists, almost so much that he releases the blood from his wrist. "They're going to kill her." The fairy flutters toward the octoman, getting into his face as though he's going to attack. "I have to get her back."

Marius grips the cane in his tentacles and slams it into the floor. "Then get her back is what we shall do, my little butterfly. Come with me and we will free her together."

Eliot looks him in the eyes. There's nothing about the octoman that he trusts, but he doesn't think he has a choice. The Naiads are the only people who can stand up to the Sylphs. Although Oona won't be happy about it, at least she will live.

"They surely must have taken her to Kaji Tower," Marius says. Then he turns to his men. "Get ready, my good gents. We're going to war."

And with those words, Eliot finds himself allied with the dirtiest, most despicable crime family in all of Grub Town.

CHAPTER
ELEVEN

Eliot gets in the backseat of Marius' Rolls-Royce and finds Avia's body, bound and gagged, her throat red from being strangled by what could have only been an octopus tentacle. It looks like she's been dead for hours.

"Sorry about the mess," Marius says as he gets into the passenger seat. "Unfortunately, some frogs have tongues that are too long for their own good."

Eliot looks at her curled up in the seat next to him. It wasn't long ago that she was talking to them, just a lowly prostitute who wanted out of her current life.

"Don't feel sorry for the poor frog," Marius says. "If it wasn't for her my sister wouldn't be in the situation she is now. Someone who's caused so much trouble does not deserve our pity."

The fairy nods, but still can't help but feel sorry for her. She was Oona's friend. Even Oona wouldn't blame her for what she did.

"So you know where Oona was taken?" Eliot asks.

Marius stretches out his tentacles across the dashboard as a shark man bodyguard takes the driver's wheel.

"Of course, I do," Marius says. "If my sister was taken to Shino Kaji there's only one place they would go. The old cunty prick never leaves his tower, thinking himself some kind of lord ruling over an empire on high. Today, we'll bring him down from his lofty pedestal. My sharks do love the taste of elf blood."

When they pull away, Eliot realizes just how many men the Naiads are taking with them. A dozen cars full of sharkmen, crabmen, and mermen speed off down the road toward the Sylph side of town. Every single one of them is thirsty for blood.

They drive uptown toward the elven penthouses where Shino Kaji resides. Eliot's never been on this side of town before, not even to pass by on the bus or in a car. It's not common for anyone but elves to venture to the world of the elven upper class. They live in tall white towers designed to look like trees, a massive forest in the center of the city. But each one is made of steel and cement, decorated with artificial branches and plastic leaves.

When the Naiads arrive, Eliot looks at the tall structures stretching overhead. It really does look like a forest, a magical forest, only the trees are larger than any that exist on Earth. The leaves are bright and colorful, shining brightly with light. Fairies, pixies and many other of the sprite races are up there, flying from tree to tree, their butts glowing like fireflies as they deliver messages and packages from one elf family to another.

"Do you have enough men?" Eliot asks when he sees the densely populated streets of elf territory. There are elf yakuza scattered everywhere through the citizenry. He can already tell they outnumber the Naiads at least fifty to one.

"Of course we don't." Marius laughs at his question. "This is Shino Kaji's territory. He's the most powerful man in the city."

Eliot looks at him with a confused face. He wonders if Oona's brother is a bit of a madman. "Then why are you just rushing in if you don't stand a chance?"

Marius turns back to him, dipping his top hat. "Just because we're outnumbered doesn't mean we don't stand a chance."

The Naiads pull up alongside the tallest tower on the block, a massive white tree-shaped building that stretches up into the heavens. The shark men from the other vehicles pile out of the car and rush for the entrance, but Marius stays back, watching his men spearhead the attack.

"There's a good reason the elves don't stand a chance against us mermen…" Marius says.

The shark men carry large rocket launchers. They go to the entrance, aiming their weapons at the entrance to the building. But once they pull the triggers, their missiles don't explode on impact. Instead, they burst into massive pools of water, as if each rocket was filled with an entire lake of salt water. The interior of the building instantly becomes flooded, the water rising up several floors. All of the elves inside don't last more than a few seconds, instantly drowning in the immense amount of water.

Marius smiles and turns back to Eliot. "Elves can't swim."

Once the building is flooded with salt water, the shark men charge and dive through the entrance, swimming through the freshly-created aquarium before the water has a chance to drain out.

"I'd like you to meet us at the top, my little butterfly," Marius says, pointing up to the upper floors of the tree-shaped tower. "That's where you'll find your darling octopus." He steps out of the car, holding out his cane as though to direct the rest of his men toward battle. He looks back for a moment and says, "If you happen to find Shino Kaji before me, you have my blessing to rip him to shreds. I will reward you greatly if you can accomplish this task."

And then the octoman slithers across the pavement, through the confused elven onlookers, toward the entrance to the flooded building.

Eliot steps out of the car and looks up. He realizes he's on his own. He can't follow the mermen through the water without drowning, so he's forced to use his wings to get up there by himself.

As elven yakuza run up the street toward him, the rest of the mermen disappearing into the flooded building, Eliot has no choice but to leap into the air and fly away. Luckily, the elves don't realize he's with the Naiads. If they fired at him, they would take him down immediately, far out of reach of his sentient blood. But, instead, they fire into the flooded lobby of the Kaji Tower, aiming at the shark men. Not a single bullet is able to reach them through the water, but the elves keep firing, hoping to do something to stop the fish men invasion.

Eliot flies high up into the sky, far beyond the eyes of those below him. But he has no idea where to go. If he entered a floor up above, it wouldn't take long for the elves to take him down. So he decides it's best to just stay out of sight, spy through the windows and wait until he finds a sign of Oona.

As he gets high enough to reach the artificial branches of the Kaji Tower, he runs into other sprites. It seems that they are part decoration for the building, like living Christmas lights, as their bodies glow with shimmering lights. They fly from branch to branch, window to window, doing an assortment of different jobs that probably range from janitorial work to prostitution. Either way, it's like a whole new ecosystem of fairykind existing far above the rest of the city.

A pixie with purple skin and black wings notices Eliot as he flutters up toward them, recognizing the fairy to be out of place.

"Hey, this is private property, twink," the pixie says, rushing toward him.

Pixies and fairies have always hated each other, ever since

the beginning of civilization. Although other races find both of them to be immensely beautiful, fairies always say that pixies smell like rotten skunk and look like ugly goblins. Pixies always say that fairies smell like rotten bananas and look like stupid bird people. It is believed that pixies are jealous that fairies are known as the more beautiful race of the two, despite how closely related they are, but others say they were created to hate each other. Opposite sides of the same coin.

"Says who, moth?" Eliot asks.

Pixies always hate being called *moths* because their wings resemble those of moths more than butterflies. They don't think they are any less beautiful than butterflies. Just because their color tends to reflect more from their skin than from their wings doesn't mean they aren't a pretty species. The pixie sneers at him, as though being called a moth is the worst insult he could have received.

"Says *me*, fairy boy," the pixie yells.

Eliot releases his blood, forming a large cloud of metal blades around him. When the pixie sees it, he just backs away.

"My mistake…" the pixie says, holding up his hands to let the fairy pass.

"Get lost," Eliot says, waving his blood toward him.

The pixie flies off toward the other sprites in the branches, leaving Eliot to do as he pleases. The moth is probably going to call for help, tell people about the rogue fairy flying up the Kaji Tower, but Eliot doesn't worry. He doesn't plan to be fluttering around for very long.

Eliot searches from window to window, looking for signs of his love. The tower is so full of windows that he can see pretty much everything from floor to floor. Everyone is in a panic within the building. He sees elven yakuza with machine guns running down the stairs, heading toward the Naiad attackers from the bottom floors. He keeps going until he gets to the top floor and sees a group of both elves and reptilians gathered there. He recognizes Madam Nuri in her gold dress. Beyond her, he sees what looks to be Oona, curled up on the floor with multiple guns pointed at her head.

There's an entrance to the room designed for sprite messengers, kind of like a doggy door for fairies. Eliot flies toward it, crawling through the flap and enters the room just enough to find out what's going on. There are too many armed men in the room for Eliot to take out on his own. Besides Madam Nuri, there are two lizard men and eight elves. Even if he could rush in and release his blood to attack the group, there's no way to prevent his blood from killing Oona in the process. He has to bide his time, wait for the right moment.

"This is your fault," one of the elves yells at the dragon lady. "The Naiads think I'm weak because of you."

"You are only weak if you are weak," Madam Nuri hisses at him.

Eliot moves closer into the room, getting a better look at the man speaking to the dragon lady. It's a tall elf in a silver suit, much older than the others. He stands with a proud yet unnerved look on his face. Eliot has no doubt that the man is Shino Kaji, the dreaded boss of the Grub Town Sylph family.

The elder elf scowls. "It doesn't matter. There's no way they can get up here. Marius is only putting the final nail in his coffin."

"I told you he would come for his sister," says Madam Nuri. "You should have just taken the fairy as I recommended. He was the one responsible for your son's death."

He turns away from her. "Marius disowned his sister long ago. Why would he go through the trouble of saving someone he loathes?"

Madam Nuri snickers at him. "Of course an elf wouldn't understand. Even if they hate each other, she's still his blood.

He wasn't going to just leave her at the hands of his enemy."

The elf grumbles at her, but doesn't respond to her comment. He pours a glass of bourbon and stews in his anger.

Then he turns to his men who hold Oona at gunpoint, "Get her out of here. Put a bullet in her head and leave her on the steps for her brother to find."

The elves bow at Shino Kaji and get Oona up from the floor. They push her toward the stairs, leading her by gunpoint. There are five of them, too many for Eliot to take on his own. He's going to have to be careful if he wants to rescue Oona without killing her in the process.

Shino Kaji looks at Madam Nuri and asks, "So you will get me the video of your snake women devouring and excreting the fairy who killed my son?"

Madam Nuri nods. "You'll have it by tomorrow."

He smiles at her. "Good. I love lamia snuff porn."

"Of course you do," Madam Nuri says. "Sadistic bastards always love to watch my girls work."

Eliot crawls outside and flutters downward, following the elves that are taking Oona to her death. The Naiads are still far below, way out of reach to save her. It's all up to him. If he can't stop the elves, she will surely die.

The elves take her down three more floors and then point their guns, aiming at the back of her head execution-style. Eliot doesn't have time to hesitate. He moves back as far as he can and then flies at the window with all of his force, trying to crash through the glass and rescue her. But he doesn't realize the glass is bulletproof until it's too late. He splats against the window, making a loud thud, stuck there like a fly on a swatter.

He watches as the elves glance over at him, confused by the presence of a little fairy pressed up against the window. Oona sees him and groans, most likely disappointed by his pathetic excuse for a rescue. Eliot looks around, desperate to get inside. He finds another messenger door and crawls toward it like a moth on glass. He pulls himself in and lets out his blood, showing off the metal blades that spiral out of his body.

The elves aren't impressed. They just watch him with cold dead eyes, as if they know he won't do anything with Oona so close to him.

"You're the octobitch's fairy boy toy aren't you?" one of the elves asks.

"Your blood won't do anything to hurt us, twink," another says. "Flutter away before we squash you."

Eliot is confused by their nonchalant behavior. He holds up his bleeding wrist, but they show no signs of being threatened by it.

"Let her go or you die," Eliot says.

One of them walks up to him and slaps him across the face with the butt of his submachine gun and then says, "Nobody is frightened of you, tiny insect. Go fly into a bug-zapper and leave us alone."

The blood flies at the elf, but he casually dodges the attack and steps out of range. Eliot is confused by how easily he escaped his blood without even a scratch. He doesn't know what else to do but continue to threaten them.

"I'm serious," Eliot says. "I'll kill you all."

But none of them seem worried, not even Oona thinks he stands a chance.

The fairy steps forward and releases more blood. It turns into shards of metal and darts toward the closest elf, but the yakuza just smacks it out of the air. Like a master samurai, he's able to deflect every ounce of the blood, repelling it back in Eliot's direction. The fairy has to duck to avoid being impaled by his own bodily fluid. When he gets upright, pulling his blood back into his body, the elves just stare at him like a pathetic creature annoying them with his presence.

Eliot doesn't know what to do if his blood doesn't work on these elves. He looks up at Oona. She glares back at him with disapproval.

"Why the fuck did you come here?" she asks him.

Eliot nearly crumbles at the sight of her, a look of anger in her eyes that he's never seen before.

"I couldn't just let you die," he says.

She gives him a dirty look. "I'm going to die anyway. I'd rather have my art survive."

Eliot is so weak compared to her, but he doesn't back down. Tears flow from his eyes as he steps toward her, holding the blood in his wrist. "I don't want either of us to die."

Oona says, "I'm pregnant. That's a death sentence for an octomaid. It doesn't matter either way to me as long as my art survives."

Tears fall down his cheeks as Oona says this. He shakes his head, can't believe she'd be so careless with her life. "If you're pregnant, I want you to have a chance to give birth. I want you to complete your lifecycle even if there's not much of it left. If I don't do whatever it takes to keep you alive that long then I don't deserve to have your art on my body."

Oona stares at him for a moment, glaring with all her rage. But then she lets out a loud groan. She pushes through the elves holding her at gunpoint and rushes toward him.

"You pretty fucking idiot," she says.

With her hands tied behind her back, she grabs him with her tentacles and wraps him up tightly, then kisses him. Eliot is so surprised with the spontaneous burst of affection that he just stands there as her tentacles slither between his wings and pull him closer. He doesn't release the pressure on his wrist as he kisses her back, her tongue sucking his lips into hers, pressing herself firmly to his body. When Oona pulls away, Eliot's lips are still pursed in the air.

"Fine," she says. "We'll survive together."

The elves look at them embracing as if the two lovers are

insane to have forgotten they are there, pointing guns at their heads.

"Have you forgotten about us?" one of the elves asks. "Neither of you are surviving anything."

Eliot looks at Oona in a panic, not sure what they should do. His blood has no impact on the elves. Oona's hands are tied behind her back. There's nothing they can do to escape.

"I'm sorry," Eliot says. "I couldn't save you."

Oona smiles at him, her tentacles slithering away from his body and spreading out across the room.

"Don't worry," she says. "They don't call me the Demon of Grub Town for nothing."

Before the elves know what's happening, Oona's tentacles swipe two submachine guns out of their hands and turn them on their owners. The bullets spray out in short bursts, cutting the elves down before they even know what's happening to them. When their bodies fall to the ground, she whips up the rest of their weapons into her tentacles and says, "Now we're ready to get out of here."

Eliot steps forward and looks at the dead elves that Oona took out in two seconds flat. He has no idea how she did it. He has no idea why she didn't sooner.

"There are hundreds of men downstairs," Eliot says. "We can't go that way."

Oona shrugs. "Think you can fly us down to the street?"

Eliot looks at her. She's three times his size. There's no way he could lift her, let alone fly them both to safety.

When he shakes his head, Oona says, "Then we fight our way out."

Eliot goes to her restrained arms behind her back, trying to untie her, but she just pushes forward as though she doesn't need them. He flutters after her and grabs her restraints, biting them off with his teeth before she continues downstairs. She might think she doesn't need them, but it's not the time to pull any punches. She has no idea what's waiting for them downstairs.

Five machine guns in her tentacles, slithering down the stairs on three, Oona unleashes a fury of bullets on the elves that get in her way. They drop before they see her, focused on the threat coming from farther down the stairwell. Eliot realizes that if they keep going they'll eventually get to the flooded floors at the bottom of the tower, they'll run into Oona's brother. Not only can Eliot not breathe in the water, but he can't face Oona if she learns that he came with the person she hates most in the world. He wants to tell her what they are walking into, but he just can't. A part of him thinks that it would be better if he lets her go without warning. Her brother is here to save her. He will surely protect her and help her get out. If she tries to avoid him out of stubbornness, out of some old grudge, she might get herself killed when he could otherwise help keep her alive.

As they go farther down the stairs, the elven troops grow in numbers. It is a whole army, gathered to kill the Naiads who have yet to show themselves.

"Get on my back," Oona says.

Eliot looks at her like she's crazy.

"Trust me," she says.

Eliot doesn't argue. He flitters into the air and wraps his tender arms around her neck. Then she leaps into the crowd of elves on the floor below, spraying them with bullets. As they fall, she whips up their guns in her remaining tentacles and fires in a circle, tearing them down before they can even get off a single round.

When she stops and lowers her weapons, Eliot sees a pile of two dozen elves lying before them. He can't believe she took them out so easily.

"Holy shit…" Eliot says. "How did you do that?"

Oona barely registers it as any kind of feat of heroics. "I was Madam Nuri's top enforcer. This is what I used to do for a living, before I was a tattooist."

Eliot can't help but be impressed. In fact, he thinks it's pretty hot.

"You're still a better tattooist than you are a killer," Eliot says.

It makes Oona smile, but only a little. She rubs one of his arms wrapped around her and kisses his tiny hand. It was the right thing for him to say.

"Let's kill more of these bastards," she says, then continues her assault down the stairwell.

Eliot thinks there's nothing that can get in her way, tearing through elf after elf, wiping them out before they even see her coming. It seems like they'll have no problems getting out of there alive until they get closer to the flooded floors of the tower. They reach a level overrun with elves, a force five times the size of the last one they came across. And on the other side of them, an army of shark men are coming out of the water, firing back at them.

"What the fuck is this…" Oona cries when she sees the Naiad forces ascending the tower.

Before she has time to think, bullets fire down at her as Shino Kaji and his men flank them from behind. Trapped in the middle of the onslaught, Oona has nowhere to go. She could make a run for it, dive into the waters and escape the elven gunmen, but then she would surely drown Eliot before they got to safety. Although he would be fine escaping out a window and getting away on his own, Oona decides instead to leave the stairwell and burst through the doors leading into the current floor.

She enters a large ballroom that just happens to be the staging area the elves were using to prepare for battle with the Naiads. When they see the octomaid slithering inside, they think she's just another fish man, even with a fairy wrapped around her back. They get to their feet and aim their weapons. Oona only has a split second to raise her tentacles and open fire.

"Look out!" Eliot cries.

But it's too late. The elves open fire as Oona shoots back. She's able to kill nine of the sixteen elves in the room, but not before two bullets hit her in the shoulder and waist. A third bullet grazes Eliot's back as Oona turns in a circle, shooting her tentacle guns in all directions. The blood from the fairy's wound sprays out in one long spiral of silver. Then it hardens into metal and cuts through the remaining elves, slicing them in half in three quick strikes.

Eliot panics when he sees his blood pouring out of his body so close to Oona. He's worried that it will attack her immediately, seeing her as the biggest threat in the room. But as the blood finishes off the last elf, it just hovers there, protecting them. It doesn't go for Oona. It treats her as a part of Eliot's body.

"What the hell are you doing?" Oona asks, getting a bit paranoid by the sentient blood hovering above her.

But Eliot is in shock. He can't believe what's happening.

"It's not attacking you," Eliot says. "It's like it thinks you're part of my body."

Oona rubs her lower abdomen. "Maybe because I have your DNA inside me."

Eliot shrugs. "Maybe…"

They trample over the elf corpses and go deeper into the ballroom, trying to find another way out. It is a large tower so there has to be more than one stairwell leading out of the place.

But before they can find another passageway, the battle

spills into the room with them. Elves and Naiads rush in, shooting at each other. The room becomes a new battleground. Oona takes them far away from the shootout, but she can't find another exit. They're trapped. Both Naiads and Sylphs block them in.

"Why the hell are the Naiads here, anyway?" Oona says. "We would have gotten away without them."

Eliot wonders if he should tell her about how he directed them this way, how it's pretty much his fault.

But instead, he just says, "They came for you."

Before she can get Eliot to explain what he means by that, she sees her brother, Marius, enter the room. He walks casually with his cane and top hat. He seems unarmed, not joining the fight by any means. With his eyes locked on Oona, he strides toward her, opening his tentacles as though he's asking for a hug.

"That motherfucker..." Oona says, staring her brother down.

But before Marius gets the chance to embrace his sister, the elves overpower the fish men. Two dozen sharks are impaled with bullets, and fall to the ground. Only four of them remain. The elves that triple their numbers come in, forcing the Naiads to get on their knees and throw down their weapons.

Marius just smiles. "Well, that didn't go as planned, did it?"

He winks over at Oona and Eliot.

Then the elves put bullets into the last of the shark men, leaving only Marius alive.

It doesn't take long before the rest of the elves in the building fill the room. And soon after them, Shino Kaji comes in, followed by Madam Nuri and her lizard man guards. Three dozen elves and no way out.

"What the hell are you doing here?" Oona asks her brother.

Marius smiles at her, standing up straight on his tentacles in the middle of his dead underlings. He says, "Hiya, Sis. I was hoping to find you here."

Oona seems angrier with him than both Shino Kaji or Madam Nuri. She wants to end his life if that's the last thing she can do. But before she can raise her guns and cut him down, Eliot pushes her tentacles away, urging her not to fire a shot.

"I kind of like your new fairy boyfriend," Marius says. "He should come work for us, once you rejoin our ranks."

Oona sneers at him, but Eliot kind of likes the octoman. He can't help but respect how the Naiad remains cool and calm in the current situation. Even though Marius is surrounded by enemies with no chance of survival, he's still acting as if nothing is wrong. Eliot wishes he had that kind of confidence. It's yet another reason why he admires octopus people so much.

"Why would I ever rejoin you?" Oona asks. "Why are you even here?"

Marius points at Eliot. "I came with your boyfriend."

When he says this, Eliot can feel the rage flowing through Oona's skin. Her eyeballs curl in the fairy's direction, looking at him over her shoulder.

Eliot's antennae curl downward. "I just wanted to save you."

Oona shakes her head. "I'm going to kick your ass so hard if we ever get out of this…"

But before they can argue any further, the elves close in, aiming their weapons at both Marius and Oona. Shino Kaji steps through the ranks of his elf army, enjoying the feeling of having the three people he wants dead most in the world right in front of him.

"This is funny…" the elf says, standing behind Marius. "The king of the mermaids comes to save his dear sister and ends up sharing her fate. Only a fish would be stupid enough to try such a thing."

"I'm an octopus, not a fish," Marius says. "We cephalopods resent when bipeds confuse us like that… especially dirty elves."

Shino Kaji points and an elf rushes in, slamming Marius in the back of the head with the butt of his gun.

Then the elf boss turns toward Eliot. "And I've also got the fairy who killed my spoiled brat of a son." He steps closer to the fairy. "I thought you would be snake shit by now."

He turns to Madam Nuri with an annoyed expression on his face. Then turns back to Eliot and Oona.

"Not to worry, though," says Shino Kaji. "I prefer having the chance to kill you myself, anyway."

Even though Eliot's blood hovers in the air above him and Oona, the head of the elf yakuza doesn't show any concern over its presence.

As he comes close, Oona raises the guns in her tentacles and fires. Half the guns are empty. The few that aren't release several rounds that all pass over the elf's head as he stands there with complete composure, not flinching for a second, not an ounce of worry in his body. The guns click and click as Oona continues triggering them, but there's no bullets left to fire, leaving her completely defenseless.

"So let me get this straight..." Shino Kaji continues, brushing the smell of gun smoke from his nose. "Bear with me, I'm an old man." He turns to Eliot. "From my understanding, my son wanted to fuck your little fairy ass and you didn't want that. It's understandable, my son was an entitled little prick who always wanted whatever he couldn't have." He paces closer to Eliot. "So he probably tried to take you by force and that's when this octopus stepped in to save you."

Eliot opens his mouth, trying to correct his story, but the Elf holds up his finger and Eliot realizes he can no longer get out any words.

Shino Kaji continues, "But the octopus was not quite enough to stop him, or maybe even didn't want to try to stop him knowing what would happen if she ever harmed anyone of Kaji blood." He points at Eliot. "So, trying to save the woman who risked her life to protect him, the fairy used his parasitic blood to kill my son and his friends." He turns to Marius. "And when they were finally captured, the octopus' brother stepped in to save her, despite the fact that she was a disloyal backstabber who preferred a dragon's warmth over her brother's swamp."

When he finishes, Shino Kaji turns to Madam Nuri. She nods her head at him. Shino turns back to Eliot and Oona, fire burning in his eyes.

"Now what I want to know is why any of you thought you could possibly survive such foolish actions," he says. "You're all pathetic races. Fucking insects and ocean trash. My son was worth a thousand of you. All of you deserve far more than death for ending his life centuries before his time."

Eliot can't believe the old elf would say such things. Niko Kaji was the biggest douchebag Eliot has ever known. He was a rapist and a scumbag. Killing him was the best thing he's ever done for society and he doesn't regret it for a second.

But before Eliot can open his mouth to tell the elf exactly how he feels, Oona says, "Your son was a piece of shit and he deserved to die."

The room goes quiet. None of them can believe Oona would say such a thing, not even Madam Nuri, not even her brother.

Shino Kaji doesn't bother arguing with the octomaid. The second she says her words, a grimace appears on his face and the elf finds himself unable to speak. He goes to one of his men and takes the gun from his hands. Then he steps toward Oona and opens fire.

Oona is sprayed with bullets, but not a single one reaches her flesh. Eliot's blood wraps around her body, forming a hard metal shield, blocking every shell from reaching her. The slugs bounce off, dropping to the floor. Everyone in the room is shocked by the occurrence, even Eliot. He has no idea why his blood protected Oona as it did. It's like his blood is trying to protect the DNA in her body, or maybe it just knows how much Oona means to him and worries that its host will commit suicide if he loses the love of his life. Or maybe it can feel Eliot's emotions flowing through his bloodstream and feels the same way as he does about the octopus woman who has chosen him to be her mate.

"That isn't going to save you," says Shino Kaji, acting confident and strong, but unable to hide being flustered by having his bullets shrugged away. "There's not enough blood in your body to save you."

The second he says this, Eliot's blood reacts. It moves as if accepting Shino Kaji's challenge. The metal blood drains out in a thick sheet, coating Oona's body. It leaks over her from head to toe, enveloping her in a three-inch layer of liquid metal. When it hardens, both Oona and Eliot are protected by an armored coating of steel.

The second he sees it, Shino Kaji backs away, getting behind his men. He orders them to attack, but their bullets just ricochet off the metal skin and bounce back at them.

Despite being as surprised by this outcome as everyone else, Oona smiles at her new protective coating and charges forward. The elves unleash a fury of bullets, but nothing can penetrate the armor, and Oona is unscathed. Her tentacles turn into long razor-sharp swords and she cuts through the elves one at a time, slicing open their throats, piercing through their abdomens, turning every one of them into Swiss cheese until none of the soldiers are left alive.

Once he's alone, Shino Kaji rushes Oona. Leaping through the air toward her, instead of focusing on the octomaid, he goes for the fairy on her back, knowing that Eliot is the source of her protection and potentially her weakness.

But before the elf can reach Eliot, Oona thrusts a tentacle above her head, impaling the elder yakuza through the stomach without even looking at him. Then she whips around and decapitates the bastard. The smug elf expression stays on Shino's face even as his head flies from his body, landing in a pool of his men's blood.

When Oona finishes her onslaught, only Marius, Madam Nuri and her two subordinates remain. She turns to them, breathing deeply through the metal armor coating her skin.

Madam Nuri raises her hands and then claps three times.

"Good for you," the dragon lady says. "You killed the son of a bitch."

Oona has blood in her eyes. Eliot can't see her, but he knows something's wrong. She has a thirst for death that can't be quenched. She goes toward Madam Nuri, raising her tentacles.

"I no longer have a need for you, Oona," Madam Nuri says, not even slightly backing down from the metal tentacles pointed in her direction. "You are free to leave my employment."

Oona charges at the dragon lady, but then pauses a meter within her reach. She doesn't follow through with her attack.

"You sold me out to protect your business," Oona says. Her words sound warbled and metallic with Eliot's blood coating her voice box.

"Of course I did," says Madam Nuri. "And I would do it again. If a woman shows weakness in the world of men, she is eaten alive. You've never been in my position, so you'd never understand. I've always seen you as a daughter, but no one in my position has the privilege of sparing even their own daughter at the cost of their business. I loved you, but you were expendable. Everyone is."

Oona screams at her and slices her two bodyguards in half, but she leaves Madam Nuri where she stands.

Madam Nuri shakes her head slowly and says, "That was an immature thing to do. I thought you were better than that."

"You can leave on your own," Oona says. "If you can hold your breath long enough to escape."

Eliot wonders if the dragon lady realizes what Oona is talking about, or if she knows that there's no way out of the building without swimming three floors.

Madam Nuri just shakes her head and says, "I don't need to escape. I'll wait for the police to arrive. They'll escort me home."

Then she turns and walks toward the exit. Oona watches the dragon's every step, her eyes narrowing at the woman she once thought of as a mother and a mentor, her expression filled with both anger and respect.

The dragon lady turns back before she leaves the room. "You proved yourself to be a worthy daughter in the end." When she looks at Oona, Eliot can almost see tears forming in her scaly eyes. "I hope your final days are happy ones."

And then she walks away, stepping over dead bodies toward the exit.

Eliot pulls his blood back into his body. The skin of metal coating Oona slides away from her tentacles, away from her arms and chest and face, and returns to the open hole in the fairy's back. Eliot puts pressure on his wound, trying to keep it all inside. He pushes back from Oona and hovers in the air, fluttering his wings.

The only other living person who remains in the room is Oona's brother, Marius. He lifts himself up on his tentacles, taps his cane on the floor and straightens his top hat as though nothing of consequence just happened.

"It's good to have all that sorted," Marius says, turning to Oona. "Now are we ready to head back home, my dear sister?" He turns to Eliot. "And my friend of fairykind?"

Although Oona no longer has Eliot's metal blood covering her body, she turns to her brother as though she's going to cut him to pieces with her tentacles.

"Why would I ever go with you?" Oona says.

Marius snickers. "Where else are you going to go? You're no longer with Madam Nuri. The other Sylph families are going to want revenge. It's time you rejoined your own kind."

Oona lunges at him and wraps a tentacle around his neck. "I told you I would kill you if I ever saw you again."

Although he's visibly choking, Marius just shrugs at her. He spews out the words, "That was all in the past."

Oona releases him and he gasps for air.

"You treated me as a tool," Oona says. "You never cared about me as a sister. All you wanted was for me to kill for you. When you had me slaughter our only surviving sibling, I told you that if I ever saw you again that you'd be next."

Marius straightens his top hat. "It couldn't be helped. You know Leo was going to turn us both in to the police. It broke my heart as much as it broke yours."

Oona glares at him. "But you weren't the one who had to kill him. You put that on me. You don't know what it was like to have to look him in the eyes when he died."

Marius points his cane at her. "Did you think I wanted that to happen? He's the one who betrayed us, not the other way around. I had to kill him to save you. You're my sister. I love you more than anyone else in the world."

"Then why did you send your men to execute me?" Oona asks.

"You waged war on the Naiads," Marius explains. "You killed several of my men. What else was I to do? I never should have had you kill Leo. I thought it would be better for him, to have someone who loved him do it instead of a stranger. But I was wrong to put that on you. You deserved better. Both of you did. You two were everything to me. I built my empire to create a safe haven for you, for all of us."

Oona turns away from him. "In the end, it just tore us apart."

Marius calms down, straightening his scarf and slithering toward his sister.

"I want to make it up to you," he says. "I know I'm a bastard. You can hate me all you want. But what's it going to take to bring you back to me?"

She doesn't respond. Out of desperation, the octoman goes to Eliot.

"Help me out here, butterfly," he says to the fairy. "You've got to know what she wants."

Eliot looks him in the eyes. He seems genuinely serious about his words. He really seems like he wants the best for his sister. Because Eliot also cares for Oona, he can't help but feel for the man.

"She just wants to live out her lifespan in peace," Eliot says.

When the octoman hears this, the expression changes on his face. He turns to his sister. She looks back at him and nods her head.

"I'm pregnant," she says.

When he hears her words, he is both upset and sympathetic.

"I'm sorry..." he says. "I mean, congratulations."

Oona turns to him. "So now that I can't be a killer for you, I assume you'll be moving on."

But Marius surprises all of them by shaking his head.

"No," he says. "Come back with me. Spend the last of your days in safety." He turns to Eliot. "Both of you. I'll protect you. I just want the best for my sister, I swear. I'll make sure you get to the ocean and give birth, finish your lifecycle. I'll do everything in my power to keep you happy until then."

Oona looks at him, then back at Eliot.

"We don't need you," she says. Then she grabs the fairy's arm with a tentacle. "Just stay the fuck away from us."

And they leave the room, climbing over the dead elves, not looking back at the octoman who stands there with a stupid look on his face, a stupid hat on his head, a stupid cane in his hand, reaching out with his tentacles as though wishing to embrace her and tell her how sorry he is for bringing so much misery into her life for so many years.

CHAPTER TWELVE

When Eliot was a little boy, he loved nothing more than going to the ocean. He would always flutter up and down at his parents, begging them to take him to the ocean again. They only lived ninety minutes away, so it wasn't that far of a trip. But they never wanted to go. He always had to put all his energy into convincing them, determined to make their lives miserable if they didn't take him to his favorite place in the world, otherwise they would refuse him.

"You know the sun is bad for fairies," his mother would always say. "It burns our wings to a crisp. It ruins our sensitive skin."

But Eliot didn't care. He wanted to go so bad. He wanted to go every weekend if he could.

"But we have to go," Eliot would always cry. "You promised we would. I'll do anything. I'll be good and do all my homework. Please…"

No matter how much they resisted, his parents would always give in. They loved their little boy so much that there's nothing in the world that they could refuse him, especially when he wanted it so much.

So they would pack a picnic of snapdragon sandwiches and sunflower soda and take their boy to the beach, allowing him to run across the sand and watch the waves.

"Don't do more than wade in the water to your ankles," his

father would always say. "If you get your wings wet you won't be able to fly away."

Eliot would always agree but he'd eventually get his wings wet anyway. He wasn't that good of a flier back then, so he never knew what the big deal was. He loved the feeling of letting the salt water drench his wings and stick them to his back. He liked how it made him look more like the other people at the beach, the humans and the elves, all the people who didn't have wings and thought he looked like an insect when they fluttered at his sides.

"Stay within our sights," his mother would always say. "Don't fly up toward the kites and get tangled up again."

And his father would add, "Don't fly out to the surfers and try to ride on the backs of their boards again."

This was several years before his parents died in a car accident and left Eliot all alone in the world. The seatbelts were designed to protect larger beings, those who were human or elf-sized. They didn't do much for fairies, especially not with their fragile bones. It was only a minor crash, but they both died instantly. Eliot was only nineteen when he was forced to endure the world without people who loved him. It was difficult for him to understand an existence so different than the one his parents introduced him to. He spent years going from one relationship to another, hoping that he could one day find something that was even slightly as comforting as the relationship he was born into. But his parents spoiled him with love. Fairies can't help but always be spoiled with love.

"Don't get too close to the waves," his mother would say. "They are so strong that they'll knock you over."

His father would add, "Watch out for crabs. They might pinch your little toes right off."

But Eliot didn't mind all of their warnings. He didn't care about playing in the waves or flying up to the kites the other kids liked to play with. What made him love the ocean so much was what he would always see within it. He would flutter up close to the water, as close as he could before the waves got too strong. Then he would look out at the three children who always swam in the waters near that spot.

Nobody else seemed to notice them, or maybe they just didn't care. But Eliot was fascinated by the children in the waves. They swam with ease, never having to worry about drowning or getting sunburns or getting their wings all wet. Whenever they flipped over to dive under the water, their octopus tentacles would snake through the air like happy little eels. There were two boys and one girl. All of them were a little older than him, but he always wanted to be their friends. He always wanted them to come to the shore and talk to him and tell them what their life was like swimming in the water all the time.

But the octopus children never left the water to be with him. He'd come every weekend and they'd always be there, visiting the shore as he would visit the beach. They seemed scared of the land, not sure what to make of it. He wished he had the courage to fly out to them and tell them that they would love it if they just came to his world and had a picnic with him and his family. If only they could taste his mother's delicious cherry blossom cookies, he knew they would want to be friends with him forever. He didn't have any friends who liked him on the land. He hoped the kids who lived in the water would be different. He hoped they would be nicer, more open to the idea of spending time with a boy with wings, a boy so much smaller than all the other boys.

It was the girl that he especially liked. She had long beautiful locks of blue hair that spread out in the water like strands of seaweed. As her brothers swam around and played in the water, she just looked out at the land with her deep dark eyes, staring across the beach as if she wanted to crawl out onto the sand and join the other kids building sand castles and flying big butterfly-shaped kites. But more than the wingless children, she seemed especially interested in the boy who had kites growing out of his back, the one who could fly without the need of wind and a string.

Every weekend, they would meet at the shore and just stare at each other. Eliot would flutter up in the air so that she could get a good look at him. She would lift her tentacles up out of the water and rub her forehead in amazement at the boy with the strange kites on his back. They would always spend the afternoon inching closer together. She would get the nerve to slither up through the waves toward the sand. He would find the bravery to disobey his parents and flutter over the water. But they were never able to meet. They never were able to get close enough to see what the other was really all about.

One day, Eliot was able to witness the girl with the octopus body climb out of the sea. She was still too far away for him to reach her, but he was able to get a good look at her as it happened. Once he saw her whole body, despite her tentacles covered in sand and salt water, Eliot realized she was the most beautiful girl he'd ever seen in the whole world. He wanted nothing more than to fly over to her and help her out of the sea, show her everything there is to love about his life on the land.

But before he was able to reach her, the lifeguards swarmed in and captured her in nets. They went after her brothers and scooped them up and took them all away. Eliot tried to stop them. He fluttered in their faces, crying at them to let them go back to the sea. But the lifeguards just swatted him away, treating him like an annoying insect, and continued to drag the octopus kids up the sand.

All Eliot could do was grab onto the net encompassing the octopus girl. She seemed so much larger up close than she did in the waves, her tentacles curled up in a ball, squirting ink all over the beach, unable to find a way out of the net. He looked into her deep black eyes and wanted to tell her how much he loved her, how much he wanted her to come home with him and be showered with affection the way his parents did to him. But the lifeguards just kicked Eliot away and then

196

moved on, dragging the children off to somewhere they didn't want to go. As they were taken away, they squealed and chirped in a language Eliot just didn't understand. He was confused when they bit and snapped at the people carrying them, acting more like animals than civilized beings. He wanted to fly after them and teach them everything he knew about the world, but his parents yelled at him to come back under the shade of the umbrella and he wasn't able to say anything to them at all.

Eliot went back to the beach every weekend after that, but he never saw the octopus children in the waves ever again. He wasn't sure why they weren't in the sea waiting for him. He didn't know why there weren't more girls with blue hair and tentacles swimming out there, curious about the world on the land. He thought a girl like that might actually want to be friends with him. She might actually see his wings as something great and wonderful rather than a freakish extension from his skinny little body.

He might have grown up since then, forgotten all about his time at the beach, but Eliot has never stopped dreaming about being with the children of the sea. Deep down, he's always known he would see them again one day.

Eliot and Oona stand on the beach, the same beach that he used to go to as a child. They've spent several months together, sharing as much time as they had left in each other's arms, but it's now time for Oona to return to the ocean.

Oona's belly is swollen with her brood of offspring, ready to release them into the depths of the sea. Eliot holds her by the hand, not wanting to let her go. His wings flutter as she slithers toward the water, almost as though trying to pull her back. But his tiny fairy body doesn't have the strength to keep her away from her destiny.

It's not until they stand in the waves on the beach that they realize they have met before, a long time ago. With all of her tattoos and hair styled in a mohawk, he never noticed she was the girl in the sea that he fell in love with when he was a small child. He never realized that it was his experience with her back then that made him want to be with her again, want her to tattoo her art all over his body, want to risk his life to save her from those who wanted her dead.

She realizes it as well, looking at the pretty kites attached to his body, standing on the sand as he did when they were children. It is the first time she admits that she's proud to have mated with Eliot in the end. She realizes that the only reason she came on land in the first place was to be with him.

"I'll be waiting for you out in the waves when your time's at an end," she tells Eliot, brushing her hand down the tattoos on his arm. "Keep yourself pretty for me."

Eliot squeezes her hand as she pulls away from him, removing herself from his grasp. But then she turns to face him. She wraps her tentacles around his quivering wings and kisses him one last time before she has to go.

When she releases him, Oona doesn't look back. She leaves Eliot standing there, his eyes closed, his lips pursed in the wind. Then she slithers through the sand toward the water. No light reflects the surface from the cold overcast sky. It's not a sunny summer day as they experienced when they met in the past.

Eliot can't take his eyes off her as she crawls into the waves and then plunges into the depths. He looks away for a moment, trying not to burst into tears. But before he turns to leave, he looks back one last time and sees her staring back at him. She looks just as she did so many years ago, the girl in the water with the wet blue hair, watching him play on the shoreline.

He steps closer, moving toward the sand, finding himself transformed back into the child he was back then. He's too frightened to move any closer to the water, just as she is too frightened to come to him on land. But both of them want more than anything for one of them to come to the other and free them from their perpetual loneliness.

The girl in the water just waits there, staring longingly at the shore as Eliot backs away, going toward the only other person on the beach.

Marius nods his top hat at Eliot as the fairy flutters toward him. He stands there with his weight on his cane and watches his sister out in the waves.

"She always loved to come and see the fairy who lived on the shore," Marius says. "It was all she ever wanted to do, back when we were young. She used to come even early in the morning and late into the night, confused by why you weren't there to greet her as you would during the day."

Eliot looks up at him, sniffing and holding back his tears.

"Sometimes two worlds are never meant to come together," Marius says, removing his hat. "No matter how much they love to watch each other from afar, bringing them together only ends with destruction."

Eliot shakes his head and lifts his sleeve, showing off the tattoos on his arm.

"The collision of two worlds is as beautiful as it is destructive," Eliot says, looking out into the sea. "I don't mind watching my world burn as long as it results in brilliant colors." He pauses for a moment. "Better than living a life in the dull darkness."

Marius lets out a sigh as Oona disappears into the water, flapping her tentacles against the waves and swimming deep into the darkest depths of the sea.

"If you ever need employment, come see me," Marius says to the fairy, placing his hat back on his head. "We're family now, the last family I have left. And I could use a butterfly as deadly as you are."

He grins at Eliot and then turns to slither away. But Eliot doesn't say goodbye to him. Although he feels comfortable knowing there's someone else in the world who cares for Oona as much as he does, Eliot knows it would be offensive to his love if he ever had anything to do with her loathsome brother, the man she refused to have anything to do with, even if it meant giving up her life.

Eliot comes back to that beach every single day, just when the sun is at its peak in the sky. He watches for children who might one day appear in the waves, just as he saw the children out there all that time ago. He knows it might take them a while to find their way back, but he plans to make sure that if they do eventually come they will be greeted by someone who has been waiting for them, someone who will show them love in the way that their half-fairy hearts long to embrace.

There's a part of him that thinks they might be afraid of him, too afraid to ever come on land to meet their father. But another part of him, the part he's put all of his faith into, believes that his children will come out of the sea because they smell the ink of their mother tattooed all over his skin. They will know that coming to him means that they will be coming home to a world filled with love. And he plans to make sure they never have to experience the darkness of the world below the ocean, or the darkness of the world on land their mother was forced to endure, for the rest of their fishy little lives.

BONUS SECTION

This is the part of the book where we would have published an afterword by the author but he insisted on drawing a comic strip instead for reasons we don't quite understand.

Thank you for reading my new book, *Full Metal Octopus.* Wasn't it tentacley?

It's me CM3!

This book was a throwback to the kind of stories I used to write about a decade ago, stuff from 2009-2013.

It was fun to write a pulp action fantasy crime story again.

Umm...

Yeah, about that...

And it's not just this book. The vast majority of your books are full of creepy sex with weird female creatures.

FULL ETAL OPUS

Hmmmm...

I didn't notice...

You've done demon sex, alien sex, mermaid sex, werewolf sex, mutant sex, cyborg sex, clown sex, now tentacle sex.

Do you have a monster girl fetish or something?

What's a monster girl fetish?

It's when you fetishize weird half-human fantasy creatures. It's gotten super popular in Japanese hentai over the past few years.

Huh... never heard of it.

Reading Monster Musume

A character shows a lot of their inner personality during intimacy. I use sex scenes to bring that out of them. But I feel like illustrating how characters deal with conflict is even more important for learning what makes them tick, so I try to add as much conflict to sex scenes as I can. The easiest way to do this is if the character is being intimate with a strange and dangerous creature who can kill him at any second. And when the sex partners aren't life-threatening black widow types, they are at least poisonous, mysterious, unstable, disgusting, antagonistic, sadistic, controlling, creepy, freaky, or all of the above.

That's why my sex scenes sometimes come across as more gross or awkward or weird than erotic. As long as there's conflict, no sex scene is gratuitous. It will always serve an important purpose to the story.

Only hacks write sex for the sake of sex.

Acting cool

Whoa... Are you serious?

Nah, I'm fucking with you.

THE
END

ABOUT THE AUTHOR

Carlton Mellick III is one of the leading authors of the bizarro fiction subgenre. Since 2001, his books have drawn an international cult following, despite the fact that they have been shunned by most libraries and chain bookstores.

He won the Wonderland Book Award for his novel, *Warrior Wolf Women of the Wasteland*, in 2009. His short fiction has appeared in *Vice Magazine, The Year's Best Fantasy and Horror #16, The Magazine of Bizarro Fiction,* and *Zombies: Encounters with the Hungry Dead*, among others. He is also a graduate of Clarion West, where he studied under the likes of Chuck Palahniuk, Connie Willis, and Cory Doctorow.

He lives in Portland, OR, the bizarro fiction mecca.

Visit him online at **www.carltonmellick.com**

QUICKSAND HOUSE

Tick and Polly have never met their parents before. They live in the same house with them, they dream about them every night, they share the same flesh and blood, yet for some reason their parents have never found the time to visit them even once since they were born. Living in a dark corner of their parents' vast crumbling mansion, the children long for the day when they will finally be held in their mother's loving arms for the first time... But that day seems to never come. They worry their parents have long since forgotten about them.

When the machines that provide them with food and water stop functioning, the children are forced to venture out of the nursery to find their parents on their own. But the rest of the house is much larger and stranger than they ever could have imagined. The maze-like hallways are dark and seem to go on forever, deranged creatures lurk in every shadow, and the bodies of long-dead children litter the abandoned storerooms. Every minute out of the nursery is a constant battle for survival. And the deeper into the house they go, the more they must unravel the mysteries surrounding their past and the world they've grown up in, if they ever hope to meet the parents they've always longed to see.

Like a survival horror rendition of *Flowers in the Attic*, Carlton Mellick III's *Quicksand House* is his most gripping and sincere work to date.

HUNGRY BUG

In a world where magic exists, spell-casting has become a serious addiction. It ruins lives, tears families apart, and eats away at the fabric of society. Those who cast too much are taken from our world, never to be heard from again. They are sent to a realm known as Hell's Bottom—a sorcerer ghetto where everyday life is a harsh struggle for survival. Porcelain dolls crawl through the alleys like rats, arcane scientists abduct people from the streets to use in their ungodly experiments, and everyone lives in fear of the aristocratic race of spider people who prey on citizens like vampires.

Told in a series of interconnected stories reminiscent of Frank Miller's *Sin City* and David Lapham's *Stray Bullets*, Carlton Mellick III's *Hungry Bug* is an urban fairy tale that focuses on the real life problems that arise within a fantastic world of magic.

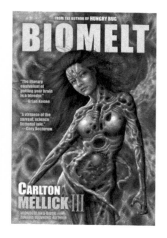

BIO MELT

Nobody goes into the Wire District anymore. The place is an industrial wasteland of poisonous gas clouds and lakes of toxic sludge. The machines are still running, the drone-operated factories are still spewing biochemical fumes over the city, but the place has lain abandoned for decades.

When the area becomes flooded by a mysterious black ooze, six strangers find themselves trapped in the Wire District with no chance of escape or rescue. Banding together, they must find a way through the sea of bio-waste before the deadly atmosphere wipes them out. But there are dark things growing within the toxic slime around them, grotesque mutant creatures that have long been forgotten by the rest of civilization. They are known only as clusters--colossal monstrosities made from the fused-together body parts of a thousand discarded clones. They are lost, frightened, and very, very hungry.

THE TERRIBLE THING THAT HAPPENS

There is a grocery store. The last grocery store in the world. It stands alone in the middle of a vast wasteland that was once our world. The open sign is still illuminated, brightening the black landscape. It can be seen from miles away, even through the poisonous red ash. Every night at the exact same time, the store comes alive. It becomes exactly as it was before the world ended. Its shelves are replenished with fresh food and water. Ghostly shoppers walk the aisles. The scent of freshly baked breads can be smelled from the rust-caked parking lot. For generations, a small community of survivors, hideously mutated from the toxic atmosphere, have survived by collecting goods from the store. But it is not an easy task. Decades ago, before the world was destroyed, there was a terrible thing that happened in this place. A group of armed men in brown paper masks descended on the shopping center, massacring everyone in sight. This horrible event reoccurs every night, in the exact same manner. And the only way the wastelanders can gather enough food for their survival is to traverse the killing spree, memorize the patterns, and pray they can escape the bloodbath in tact.

THE BIG MEAT

In the center of the city once known as Portland, Oregon, there lies a mountain of flesh. Hundreds of thousands of tons of rotting flesh. It has filled the city with disease and dead-lizard stench, contaminated the water supply with its greasy putrid fluids, clogged the air with toxic gasses so thick that you can't leave your house without the aid of a gas mask. And no one really knows quite what to do about it. A thousand-man demolition crew has been trying to clear it out one piece at a time, but after three months of work they've barely made a dent. And then there's the junkies who have started burrowing into the monster's guts, searching for a drug produced by its fire glands, setting back the excavation even longer.

It seems like the corpse will never go away. And with the quarantine still in place, we're not even allowed to leave. We're stuck in this disgusting rotten hell forever.

EVERTIMEWEMEETATTHEDAIRYQUEEN, YOUR WHOLE FUCKING FACE EXPLODES

Ethan is in love with the weird girl in school. The one with the twitchy eyes and spiders in her hair. The one who can't sit still for even a minute and speaks in an odd squeaky voice. The one they call Spiderweb.

Although she scares all the other kids in school, Ethan thinks Spiderweb is the cutest, sweetest, most perfect girl in the world. But there's a problem. Whenever they go on a date at the Dairy Queen, her whole fucking face explodes. He's not sure why it happens. She just gets so excited that pressure builds under her skin. Then her face bursts, spraying meat and gore across the room, her eyeballs and lips landing in his strawberry sundae.

At first, Ethan believes he can deal with his girlfriend's face-exploding condition. But the more he gets to know her, the weirder her condition turns out to be. And as their relationship gets serious, Ethan realizes that the only way to make it work is to become just as strange as she is.

EXERCISE BIKE

There is something wrong with Tori Manetti's new exercise bike. It is made from flesh and bone. It eats and breathes and poops. It was once a billionaire named Darren Oscarson who underwent years of cosmetic surgery to be transformed into a human exercise bike so that he could live out his deepest sexual fantasy. Now Tori is forced to ride him, use him as a normal piece of exercise equipment, no matter how grotesque his appearance.

SPIDER BUNNY

Only Petey remembers the Fruit Fun cereal commercials of the 1980s. He remembers how warped and disturbing they were. He remembers the lumpy-shaped cartoon children sitting around a breakfast table, eating puffy pink cereal brought to them by the distortedly animated mascot, Berry Bunny. The characters were creepier than the Sesame Street Humpty Dumpty, freakier than Mr. Noseybonk from the old BBC show Jigsaw. They used to give him nightmares as a child. Nightmares where Berry Bunny would reach out of the television and grab him, pulling him into her cereal bowl to be eaten by the demented cartoon children.

When Petey brings up Fruit Fun to his friends, none of them have any idea what he's talking about. They've never heard of the cereal or seen the commercials before. And they're not the only ones. Nobody has ever heard of it. There's not even any information about Fruit Fun on google or wikipedia. At first, Petey thinks he's going crazy. He wonders if all of those commercials were real or just false memories. But then he starts seeing them again. Berry Bunny appears on his television, promoting Fruit Fun cereal in her squeaky unsettling voice. And the next thing Petey knows, he and his friends are sucked into the cereal commercial and forced to survive in a surreal world populated by cartoon characters made flesh.

SWEET STORY

Sally is an odd little girl. It's not because she dresses as if she's from the Edwardian era or spends most of her time playing with creepy talking dolls. It's because she chases rainbows as if they were butterflies. She believes that if she finds the end of the rainbow then magical things will happen to her--leprechauns will shower her with gold and fairies will grant her every wish. But when she actually does find the end of a rainbow one day, and is given the opportunity to wish for whatever she wants, Sally asks for something that she believes will bring joy to children all over the world. She wishes that it would rain candy forever. She had no idea that her innocent wish would lead to the extinction of all life on earth.

Sweet Story is a children's book gone horribly wrong. What starts as a cute, charming tale of rainbows and wishes soon becomes a vicious, unrelenting tale of survival in an inhospitable world full of cannibals and rapists. The result is one of the darkest comedies you'll read all year, told with the wit and style you've come to expect from a Mellick novel.

AS SHE STABBED ME GENTLY IN THE FACE

Oksana Maslovskiy is an award-winning artist, an internationally adored fashion model, and one of the most infamous serial killers this country has ever known. She enjoys murdering pretty young men with a nine-inch blade, cutting them open and admiring their delicate insides. It's the only way she knows how to be intimate with another human being. But one day she meets a victim who cannot be killed. His name is Gabriel—a mysterious immortal being with a deep desire to save Oksana's soul. He makes her a deal: if she promises to never kill another person again, he'll become her eternal murder victim.

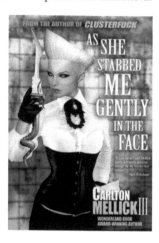

What at first seems like the perfect relationship for Oksana quickly devolves into a living nightmare when she discovers that Gabriel enjoys being killed by her just a little too much. He turns out to be obsessive, possessive, and paranoid that she might be murdering other men behind his back. And because he is unkillable, it's not going to be easy for Oksana to get rid of him.

TUMOR FRUIT

Eight desperate castaways find themselves stranded on a mysterious deserted island. They are surrounded by poisonous blue plants and an ocean made of acid. Ravenous creatures lurk in the toxic jungle. The ghostly sound of crying babies can be heard on the wind.

Once they realize the rescue ships aren't coming, the eight castaways must band together in order to survive in this inhospitable environment. But survival might not be possible. The air they breathe is lethal, there is no shelter from the elements, and the only food they have to consume is the colorful squid-shaped tumors that grow from a mentally disturbed woman's body.

CUDDLY HOLOCAUST

Teddy bears, dollies, and little green soldiers—they've all had enough of you. They're sick of being treated like playthings for spoiled little brats. They have no rights, no property, no hope for a future of any kind. You've left them with no other option-in order to be free, they must exterminate the human race.

Julie is a human girl undergoing reconstructive surgery in order to become a stuffed animal. Her plan: to infiltrate enemy lines in order to save her family from the toy death camps. But when an army of plushy soldiers invade the underground bunker where she has taken refuge, Julie will be forced to move forward with her plan despite her transformation being not entirely complete.

ARMADILLO FISTS

A weird-as-hell gangster story set in a world where people drive giant mechanical dinosaurs instead of cars.

Her name is Psycho June Howard, aka Armadillo Fists, a woman who replaced both of her hands with living armadillos. She was once the most bloodthirsty fighter in the world of illegal underground boxing. But now she is on the run from a group of psychotic gangsters who believe she's responsible for the death of their boss. With the help of a stegosaurus driver named Mr. Fast Awesome—who thinks he is God's gift to women even though he doesn't have any arms or legs--June must do whatever it takes to escape her pursuers, even if she has to kill each and every one of them in the process.

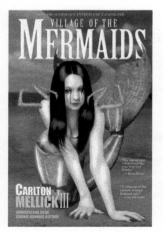

VILLAGE OF THE MERMAIDS

Mermaids are protected by the government under the Endangered Species Act, which means you aren't able to kill them even in self-defense. This is especially problematic if you happen to live in the isolated fishing village of Siren Cove, where there exists a healthy population of mermaids in the surrounding waters that view you as the main source of protein in their diet.

The only thing keeping these ravenous sea women at bay is the equally-dangerous supply of human livestock known as Food People. Normally, these "feeder humans" are enough to keep the mermaid population happy and well-fed. But in Siren Cove, the mermaids are avoiding the human livestock and have returned to hunting the frightened local fishermen. It is up to Doctor Black, an eccentric representative of the Food People Corporation, to investigate the matter and hopefully find a way to correct the mermaids' new eating patterns before the remaining villagers end up as fish food. But the more he digs, the more he discovers there are far stranger and more dangerous things than mermaids hidden in this ancient village by the sea.

I KNOCKED UP SATAN'S DAUGHTER

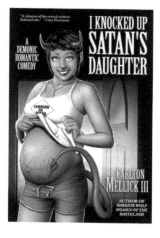

Jonathan Vandervoo lives a carefree life in a house made of legos, spending his days building lego sculptures and his nights getting drunk with his only friend—an alcoholic sumo wrestler named Shoji. It's a pleasant life with no responsibility, until the day he meets Lici. She's a soul-sucking demon from hell with red skin, glowing eyes, a forked tongue, and pointy red devil horns... and she claims to be nine months pregnant with Jonathan's baby.

Now Jonathan must do the right thing and marry the succubus or else her demonic family is going to rip his heart out through his ribcage and force him to endure the worst torture hell has to offer for the rest of eternity. But can Jonathan really love a fire-breathing, frog-eating, cold-blooded demoness? Or would eternal damnation be preferable? Either way, the big day is approaching. And once Jonathan's conservative Christian family learns their son is about to marry a spawn of Satan, it's going to be all-out war between demons and humans, with Jonathan and his hell-born bride caught in the middle.

KILL BALL

In a city where everyone lives inside of plastic bubbles, there is no such thing as intimacy. A husband can no longer kiss his wife. A mother can no longer hug her children. To do this would mean instant death. Ever since the disease swept across the globe, we have become isolated within our own personal plastic prison cells, rolling aimlessly through rubber streets in what are essentially man-sized hamster balls.

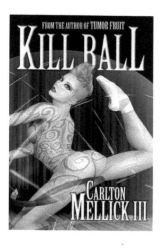

Colin Hinchcliff longs for the touch of another human being. He can't handle the loneliness, the confinement, and he's horribly claustrophobic. The only thing keeping him going is his unrequited love for an exotic dancer named Siren, a woman who has never seen his face, doesn't even know his name. But when The Kill Ball, a serial slasher in a black leather sphere, begins targeting women at Siren's club, Colin decides he has to do whatever it takes in order to protect her... even if he has to break out of his bubble and risk everything to do it.

THE TICK PEOPLE

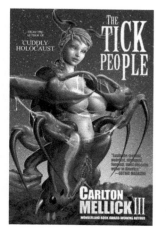

They call it Gloom Town, but that isn't its real name. It is a sad city, the saddest of cities, a place so utterly depressing that even their ales are brewed with the most sorrow-filled tears. They built it on the back of a colossal mountain-sized animal, where its woeful citizens live like human fleas within the hairy, pulsing landscape. And those tasked with keeping the city in a state of constant melancholy are the Stressmen—a team of professional sadness-makers who are perpetually striving to invent new ways of causing absolute misery.

But for the Stressman known as Fernando Mendez, creating grief hasn't been so easy as of late. His ideas aren't effective anymore. His treatments are more likely to induce happiness than sadness. And if he wants to get back in the game, he's going to have to relearn the true meaning of despair.

THE HAUNTED VAGINA

It's difficult to love a woman whose vagina is a gateway to the world of the dead...

Steve is madly in love with his eccentric girlfriend, Stacy. Unfortunately, their sex life has been suffering as of late, because Steve is worried about the odd noises that have been coming from Stacy's pubic region. She says that her vagina is haunted. She doesn't think it's that big of a deal. Steve, on the other hand, completely disagrees.

When a living corpse climbs out of her during an awkward night of sex, Stacy learns that her vagina is actually a doorway to another world. She persuades Steve to climb inside of her to explore this strange new place. But once inside, Steve finds it difficult to return... especially once he meets an oddly attractive woman named Fig, who lives within the lonely haunted world between Stacy's legs.

THE CANNIBALS OF CANDYLAND

There exists a race of cannibals who are made out of candy. They live in an underground world filled with lollipop forests and gumdrop goblins. During the day, while you are away at work, they come above ground and prowl our streets for food. Their prey: your children. They lure young boys and girls to them with their sweet scent and bright colorful candy coating, then rip them apart with razor sharp teeth and claws.

When he was a child, Franklin Pierce witnessed the death of his siblings at the hands of a candy woman with pink cotton candy hair. Since that day, the candy people have become his obsession. He has spent his entire life trying to prove that they exist. And after discovering the entrance to the underground world of the candy people, Franklin finds himself venturing into their sugary domain. His mission: capture one of them and bring it back, dead or alive.

THE EGG MAN

It is a survival of the fittest world where humans reproduce like insects, children are the property of corporations, and having a ten-foot tall brain is a grotesque sexual fetish.

Lincoln has just been released into the world by the Georges Organization, a corporation that raises creative types. A Smell, he has little prospect of succeeding as a visual artist. But after he moves into the Henry Building, he meets Luci, the weird and grimy girl who lives across the hall. She is a Sight. She is also the most disgusting woman Lincoln has ever met. Little does he know, she will soon become his muse.

Now Luci's boyfriend is threatening to kill Lincoln, two rival corporations are preparing for war, and Luci is dragging him along to discover the truth about the mysterious egg man who lives next door. Only the strongest will survive in this tale of individuality, love, and mutilation.

APESHIT

Apeshit is Mellick's love letter to the great and terrible B-horror movie genre. Six trendy teenagers (three cheerleaders and three football players) go to an isolated cabin in the mountains for a weekend of drinking, partying, and crazy sex, only to find themselves in the middle of a life and death struggle against a horribly mutated psychotic freak that just won't stay dead. Mellick parodies this horror cliché and twists it into something deeper and stranger. It is the literary equivalent of a grindhouse film. It is a splatter punk's wet dream. It is perhaps one of the most fucked up books ever written.

If you are a fan of Takashi Miike, Evil Dead, early Peter Jackson, or Eurotrash horror, then you must read this book.

CLUSTERFUCK

A bunch of douchebag frat boys get trapped in a cave with subterranean cannibal mutants and try to survive not by using their wits but by following the bro code...

From master of bizarro fiction Carlton Mellick III, author of the international cult hits Satan Burger and Adolf in Wonderland, comes a violent and hilarious B movie in book form. Set in the same woods as Mellick's splatterpunk satire Apeshit, Clusterfuck follows Trent Chesterton, alpha bro, who has come up with what he thinks is a flawless plan to get laid. He invites three hot chicks and his three best bros on a weekend of extreme cave diving in a remote area known as Turtle Mountain, hoping to impress the ladies with his expert caving skills.

But things don't quite go as Trent planned. For starters, only one of the three chicks turns out to be remotely hot and she has no interest in him for some inexplicable reason. Then he ends up looking like a total dumbass when everyone learns he's never actually gone caving in his entire life. And to top it all off, he's the one to get blamed once they find themselves lost and trapped deep underground with no way to turn back and no possible chance of rescue. What's a bro to do? Sure he could win some points if he actually tried to save the ladies from the family of unkillable subterranean cannibal mutants hunting them for their flesh, but fuck that. No slam piece is worth that amount of effort. He'd much rather just use them as bait so that he can save himself.

THE BABY JESUS BUTT PLUG

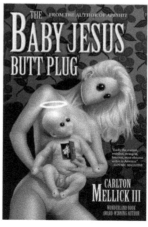

Step into a dark and absurd world where human beings are slaves to corporations, people are photocopied instead of born, and the baby jesus is a very popular anal probe.